Looking from the devastation to Tori, he noticed she was shaking.

Her face contorted as tears spilled onto her cheeks.

"Tori?" When he set an arm around her shoulders, she turned into him, sobbing.

He held her close, letting her cry, whispering words meant to soothe, though likely not helping at all. Tori was more than his sister-in-law; she was his friend. And while his brother routinely left Tori alone to handle whatever life threw her way, Micah couldn't bring himself to do that. Not now, not ever.

As sorrow continued to wrack her body, Micah ached for his friend. Longed to take away her pain. Yet for as much as it aggrieved him to see her like this, he also knew it marked the beginning of the healing process. A process that could take months, even years.

But she wouldn't have to do it alone. No matter how uncomfortable it might make him, Micah would do whatever it took to see Tori and Aiden happy again.

Publishers Weekly bestselling author **Mindy Obenhaus** lives on a ranch in Texas with her husband, two sassy pups, and countless cattle and deer. She's passionate about touching readers with biblical truths in an entertaining, and sometimes adventurous, manner. When she's not writing, you'll usually find her in the kitchen, spending time with family or roaming the ranch. She'd love to connect with you via her website, mindyobenhaus.com.

Books by Mindy Obenhaus

Love Inspired

Hope Crossing

The Cowgirl's Redemption
A Christmas Bargain
Loving the Rancher's Children
Her Christmas Healing
Hidden Secrets Between Them
Rediscovering Christmas

Bliss, Texas

A Father's Promise
A Brother's Promise
A Future to Fight For
Their Yuletide Healing

Rocky Mountain Heroes

Their Ranch Reunion
The Deputy's Holiday Family
Her Colorado Cowboy
Reunited in the Rockies
Her Rocky Mountain Hope

Visit the Author Profile page at LoveInspired.com for more titles.

Rediscovering Christmas

MINDY OBENHAUS

LOVE INSPIRED

INSPIRATIONAL ROMANCE

LOVE INSPIRED®
INSPIRATIONAL ROMANCE

Recycling programs
for this product may
not exist in your area.

ISBN-13: 978-1-335-93692-9

Rediscovering Christmas

Copyright © 2024 by Melinda Obenhaus

Love Inspired
22 Adelaide St. West, 41st Floor
Toronto, Ontario M5H 4E3, Canada
www.LoveInspired.com

Printed in Lithuania

MIX
Paper | Supporting
responsible forestry
FSC® C021394

Wherein ye greatly rejoice, though now for a season, if need be, ye are in heaviness through manifold temptations: That the trial of your faith, being much more precious than of gold that perisheth, though it be tried with fire, might be found unto praise and honour and glory at the appearing of Jesus Christ.
—*1 Peter* 1:6–7

For Your Glory, Lord

Acknowledgments

Thank You, Lord, that You are with me,
that You take hold of my right hand and tell me,
"Do not fear, for I will help you." I will praise Your name.

Chapter One

Tori Stallings could hardly wait to get home Sunday afternoon. The two gallons of airy blue-gray paint tucked in the back seat of her Ford Escape would soon coat the walls of her newly renovated kitchen, the perfect complement to the white cabinets and marble-look, solid-surface countertops that had been installed just before school had started almost a month ago.

Maneuvering her vehicle around a curve on the farm-to-market road, she tried not to dwell on the fact that the project should've been completed in July, which would have given her the remainder of her summer break to put the finishing touches on the space before heading back to a classroom full of third graders in August.

Oh, well. It was what it was. All in God's timing. After all, she'd been living in her late parents' house for years now. It was the only home her son, Aiden, had ever known. Still, the kitchen transformation had marked her first step in making the house she'd grown up in their own. After almost a decade of adjusting to change—the loss of her mother, the birth of a child, and the loss of her husband—it was time to focus on herself and Aiden. Creating a home for them, instead of just existing there. At least she should be able to have things completed in time for Aiden's birthday party in a few weeks.

She shook her head. How was it possible her baby was about to turn six?

Thankfully, Aiden had gone home with her mother-in-law, Peggy, after church today and was probably wearing himself out in the swimming pool with his uncle Micah. That should give Tori enough time to get a good head start on her project before Aiden returned.

Through her sunglasses, she scanned the horizon, spotting a column of what looked like smoke billowing into the air somewhere in the distance. As windy as it was today, that was not a good thing, especially with the summer they'd had. Temperatures had been near, at, or above the century mark since June and rainfall had been sparse all year. Pastures were brown and barren, forcing ranchers to either sell off cattle or bring in hay to feed their herds.

Since Micah, her brother-in-law, was a member of the Hope Crossing Volunteer Fire Department, he was likely on the scene, so Tori pressed the button on her steering wheel to call Peggy in hopes of finding out what was going on.

Two rings later. "Hello, Tori."

"I see smoke in the distance. Any idea what's going on?"

"Micah took off shortly after lunch. I can't see anything from our place, but word is it's somewhere west of town."

That was why she'd called. Because she lived west of town.

Ignoring the slight stutter of her heart she said, "Have you heard from him at all since then?"

"No, I haven't."

That had to be good news, right? Micah would've called if her home was in danger. After all, he wasn't just her brother-in-law. They'd been best friends since elementary school.

She released a tiny sigh of relief. "In that case, I'm going to go on home and see if I can't knock out a little bit of painting before I come and get Aiden, if that's all right with you."

"Of course, it is. He's playing in the pool with Jeremy and Trevor. Hank brought them over." Hank was Peggy's beau and the twins were his grandsons.

"I'm sure the three of them are having a ball." Tori approached the one and only stoplight in Hope Crossing, Texas, her gaze again drawn to that smoke cloud. "Call if you need me."

"Will do, hon."

Tori continued through town, her unease mounting the farther west she drove. That was some serious smoke. Arching across the otherwise blue sky, it appeared to grow increasingly dark. Yet as the road curved left and right, getting a good sense of its exact location proved difficult.

She white-knuckled the steering wheel, a sour taste filling her mouth as an invisible weight settled on her chest. *God, please let my house be okay.*

Her phone rang and when Micah's name appeared on her dash, she promptly answered. "Micah? What's going on with that fire?"

"Where are you?"

"A few minutes from my house." She spotted flashing lights up ahead. "What's happening?"

"I'll meet you as quick as I can."

"Where—" The line went dead.

Trying not to panic, she approached her turn, only to find it blocked by two sheriff's vehicles. Beyond them, half a dozen red-and-white trucks in various shapes and sizes bearing the fire department's insignia sat at the ready, while firefighters in their turnout gear gathered nearby.

Breathe, Tori. Just breathe.

She pulled up as close as she could and rolled down her window. The afternoon heat slithered into the air-conditioned space as Deputy Brady James—Hank's son and Jeremy and Trevor's father, not to mention an old schoolmate of hers—approached. "Brady, I need to get home."

Sweat trailed from his brow onto his cheek. "Sorry, Tori. Not without an escort."

"What do you mean an escort?" Removing her sunglasses, she noticed a red pickup truck with flashing emergency lights rapidly approaching from the opposite side of the blockade.

Seconds later, it came to a stop and Micah emerged from the passenger side wearing his own turnout gear. After saying something to Brady, he continued toward her. "You've got ten minutes, Tori."

Ten minutes for what?

One of the sheriff's vehicles moved out of the way while Micah hurried around to the passenger side of her SUV and threw himself into the front seat.

"Go!" The intensity in his voice was hard to miss. She'd known Micah since she was a little girl and had never heard him speak with such urgency. That could only mean one thing. This was bad. Really bad.

Myriad emotions threatened to overtake her yet she somehow managed to propel her vehicle down the narrow road, her gaze darting to the ominous cloud of smoke trailing in their direction.

"I'm not messin' around, Tori. That wildfire is out of control, so no more than ten minutes. Less if the wind picks up. Grab only what you need. And I suggest you know what that is before we get there."

"How am I supposed to do that?" Her words were high-pitched and sharper than she'd intended. "I grew up in that house."

"What's irreplaceable?"

"All of it."

"You can buy more clothes and household items."

She gulped, her palms growing sweaty as she neared the five acres dotted with pine trees where her sage-green Folk Victorian sat, the front yard surrounded by a white picket fence that matched the house's trim.

Think, Tori! You can do this. You have *to do this.*

"Photo albums. Important documents. My mother's jewelry chest. Both of our wedding rings and countless other items are in it."

"You grab the jewelry chest," Micah insisted. "Photo albums still on the shelves in the living room?"

"Yes."

"I'll get those. What about the documents?"

"They're in a fireproof box in my bedroom closet."

"Can you carry it?"

"Yes." Coming to a stop in front of the house that had been in her family for three generations, she shifted into Park, grabbed her keys and raced out of the vehicle, not bothering to close the door.

The wind caught the skirt of her sundress and the smell of smoke touched her nostrils as she pushed through the gate to charge up the front steps. Her heart had never hammered with such ferocity. Not when she'd gotten word that Joel had been killed in action or when she'd stood on the tarmac waiting for his flag-draped coffin to be carried off the plane.

When she fumbled for her house key, Micah reached for her hand. "Here, let me help you."

Once inside the living room, she made a quick right into

her bedroom. Spotting her flip-flops, she quickly swapped them for the high-heeled sandals she'd worn to church and then snagged up yesterday's T-shirt and shorts that had been beside them on the floor. Turning, she hastily gathered the carved wooden box inlaid with pearl and her parents' wedding photo alongside it atop the marble-topped antique dresser. She supposed she'd have to leave her grandmother's dresser behind.

Grief nearly overwhelmed her as she glanced around the remainder of the space with its queen-size bed and the rocking chair where she'd spent many a sleepless night with an infant Aiden. She'd lost so much already. Her parents, her husband. Surely, God wouldn't take their home, too.

"Come on, Tori!" Swiveling, she saw Micah making his way out the door, his arms full of photo albums, both old and new.

"Right behind you." She retrieved the fireproof box from her closet and started to follow him but reversed course and moved through the living space to pause at the opening to her beautiful new kitchen. She swallowed around the sudden lump in her throat. This couldn't be happening.

Squaring her shoulders, she turned, noting the triangular-shaped flag case on the mantel. The one that bore the flag they'd given her at Joel's funeral almost four years ago.

"Tori! Now!" Micah's emphatic voice as he entered once again jolted her. He took the document box from her. "Let's go."

While he started for the door, she rushed to grab the flag case, holding it close as she followed him out the door and to her vehicle where the hatch sat open.

Depositing the items into her SUV, she said, "I want the rocking chair in my bedroom."

"Sorry, Tori." Micah eyed the increasingly ominous sky. "We're out of time."

"You said ten minutes!"

"Wind's picking up." His dark eyes, so like his brother's and her son's, bore into hers. "It's time to go, Tori."

Sweat trailed down her back as she gazed at the beautiful old house that had been her home for all but a couple of her thirty-six years, feeling much the way she had when she'd kissed Joel goodbye before his final deployment. As though this was the end and her life was about to change dramatically. She could only pray she was wrong.

As sunrise approached the next morning, the smell of smoke still hung in the air. Micah lay in the middle of the road alongside some of his fellow firefighters, his body craving a few minutes of rest. It had been a long time since he'd battled a blaze so intense, not since his days as a firefighting specialist in the marines. Between the wind, parched land and Loblolly pines that had gone up like Roman candles, there'd been little they could do.

Thankfully, volunteer fire departments from across the area had joined them, bringing additional manpower and water trucks. The forest service had flown helicopters over the area, dropping water on the most intense sections. They'd also brought in bulldozers to cut firebreaks through some of the more heavily wooded areas.

Their saving grace had come after sunset, though, when the winds had begun to die down, allowing the crews to finally bring the fire under control. But not before it had burned a couple thousand acres of land, destroying dozens of homes and outbuildings in its path. Including Tori's house. Incinerated by the intense heat, it was a complete loss.

Now Micah had to break the news to her. And he couldn't

even begin to fathom how that conversation would go. Tori was a strong woman. A Gold Star wife. But everyone had their breaking point. Micah could only pray this wouldn't be Tori's. She had a lifetime of memories in that house. Lord willing, those memories would give her the courage to move forward.

Then there was Aiden. Kids were resilient, or so Micah had heard it said. Still, this was bound to impact his nephew in some way, perhaps robbing him of his sense of security. At least he still had his mama. That was what mattered most. Things could be replaced, people could not.

The sound of tires on the pavement had him opening his eyes, only to be blinded by headlights. Squinting, Micah watched as Chief Henesy approached the slow-moving pickup truck.

Moments later, the chief moved to the front of the vehicle and cupped his hands around his mouth. "Coffee and breakfast are ready when you are."

Micah pushed to his feet. Though people had been dropping off donations of water, sports drinks and food at the command post since yesterday afternoon, he hadn't had anything substantial since lunch yesterday. And his body was feeling it. He hoped there was some sort of protein to go with that coffee.

Thankfully, the breakfast tacos donated by Plowman's, the local farm supply store that also boasted a great bakery, were chock-full of eggs, sausage and cheese. And as the sun inched above the horizon, Micah was feeling much more alert.

"Good work last night, Stallings." The chief clamped a hand on Micah's shoulder. "I could tell you were in your element, helping out some of the less experienced fellas."

An element he'd found himself missing more and more

over the past year. So much so that he'd recently applied for an instructor position at the TEEX—Texas A&M Engineering Extension Service—Brayton Fire Training Field in College Station. Not that he disliked his job as a high school history teacher, he just didn't have the same passion for it that he did for firefighting.

"Thank you, sir." After a decade and a half in the military, Micah was all too familiar with working as a team.

"Sorry we couldn't save your sister-in-law's place. Those winds had us feeling downright helpless out there."

Micah nodded. "It was an act of God, pure and simple. There's nothing we could've done differently."

The chief eyed him. "Have you told her yet?"

"No." He stared into the lukewarm coffee remaining in his cup, hoping no one else had either. News traveled fast in a small town. "Some things are best said in person."

"In that case—" the chief nodded "—there's a truck headed back to the station. Why don't you go with them and head on home?"

Micah lifted a brow. "You sure?"

The chief nodded. "Go home and get some rest. We'll call if we need you."

Rest was what Micah needed. He'd contacted his principal last night, making him aware of the situation so they could find a substitute to cover his classes today. But before Micah could think about sleeping, he had to break the news to Tori, who'd gone to his mother's after leaving him yesterday. Aiden already had his own room there and the guest room with its private bath would be suitable for Tori.

"Thank you, sir." Micah downed the rest of his coffee, recalling the fear in Tori's cornflower-blue eyes as she'd given her house a final glance before leaving yesterday. He sighed. He hated being the bearer of bad news.

On the ride to the station, he contemplated just how to tell her. Not that it did much good. There was nothing he could say that would lessen the impact of the truth.

When they arrived at the brick building that also housed city hall and the library, he shrugged out of his gear and grabbed a quick shower to wash off the soot, sweat and smoke smell before climbing in his truck to make his way home to the farm.

Nowadays, he supposed calling the eight acres two miles outside Hope Crossing with a three-thousand-square-foot house and pool "a farm" was a bit of a misnomer. But back when he and his brother were growing up, countless animals had roamed the place. With him and Joel both in the FFA—something that'd been almost mandatory in the rural community with many a future farmer—rabbits, goats, sheep and heifers were commonplace. So even though their dad was a project manager turned vice president of a commercial construction firm, they preferred the idea of living on a farm.

After starting the engine, he cranked up the air-conditioning. He expected his mom would insist Tori and Aiden remain at her house for as long as necessary. But being in the same house with Tori and Aiden day in and day out? Well, Micah had better gird himself. Because while they may be the best of friends, too much time together could have his feelings crossing that fine line between friendship and something more, the way they had back in high school. Before his brother, Joel, swept her off her feet. Thankfully, Micah had never told Tori how he felt.

He glanced at the time on the dash. It was after eight. Had Tori and Aiden gone on to school? Tori taught third grade, while Aiden was in kindergarten. Micah sure would hate for Tori to learn about her house from someone else. If she was gone, he'd just have to go on up to the elementary school, because there was no telling how she'd react to the news.

Pulling out of the parking lot, he used the truck's hands-free to call his mother.

"Micah, we've been hoping to hear from you."

"I guess that means Tori is with you?"

"Yes. She didn't get much sleep last night."

Understandable. "And Aiden?"

"I took him on to school. Just got back home. Is the fire out? Are you on your way home?"

"It's contained, and yes. So there'd better be some coffee waiting for me."

"Can you tell me anything?" His mother had lowered her voice and he could only assume it was so Tori wouldn't hear her.

"I'd rather wait until I get home."

"In that case, we'll see you soon."

He pulled into the drive ten minutes later. And as he turned off the vehicle and opened the door, he spotted Tori exiting the kitchen at the back of the house. Wearing a T-shirt and denim shorts, she continued toward him, her flip-flops making that familiar slapping noise with each determined step.

With a deep breath, he placed a booted foot onto the concrete drive and stood. The day had barely started and the sun was already intense. It was going to be another scorcher, all right.

Tori stopped in front of him, and he couldn't help noticing the dark circles rimming her pretty blue eyes. Not to mention the lines pleating the normally smooth skin on her forehead. The typically fresh-faced quintessential girl next door looked as though she'd been through the wringer. And he hated that he was about to make things worse.

"How bad is it?" Bloodshot eyes met his. Her bottom lip trembled.

He sucked in a breath. "Why don't we go inside?"

"No!" Fists balled at her sides, she glared at him. "I've been waiting all night. I want to know about my house."

He felt his shoulders sag. "I'm sorry, Tori. It's a complete loss."

Wincing, she took a step back. "Complete—" She shook her head. "That can't be. That…that's my house. It can't be—" she brought a shaky hand to her mouth "—*gone.*" Her face contorted then.

He lunged for her as she crumpled. Scooping her into his arms, he carried her to the house. For a grown woman, she sure didn't weigh much.

His mother held the kitchen door open as they approached. "Take her into the living room."

He veered right, into the dining room, continuing through it to the living room with its cathedral ceiling, stone fireplace and vinyl plank flooring he'd installed last year. Approaching the floral sofa, he found himself torn. Should he lay Tori down or keep holding her? She was his friend, after all. If she was grieving—which she definitely was—he wanted to offer her whatever comfort he could.

Turning, he opted to sit, still holding her in his arms as tears streamed down her cheeks, dampening the front of his T-shirt. Boy, was he glad Aiden was at school. Seeing his poor mama this upset could really do a number on a kid.

"Oh, Tori." Mom was beside him now. She smoothed a hand over Tori's blond waves, her silver-blue eyes fixed on him as though looking for answers.

Lips pursed, he simply shook his head.

He had no idea how long the three of them sat there. None of them spoke because there'd been nothing to say.

There was no room for platitudes at a time like this. He was certain Tori would hear her fair share of those over the coming days, weeks and months. But he and his mom cared about her too much for that. Sometimes the best thing you could do was to let someone cry.

Like the night of her mother's funeral when he'd visited Tori to see how she was doing. It still angered him that Joel hadn't been there for her. Instead of arranging things so he could attend the funeral, his brother had come home two weeks later after the worst of Tori's grief had begun to ease. His presence had only sent her back into the throes of sorrow. Especially when he'd left five days later. At least, according to their mother.

Now, as Tori began another grieving process, Micah prayed for his friend. Pleaded with God to take away her pain and give her a glimmer of hope. Yet as sobs racked her body, Micah was all too aware it was going to be a long, sorrowful journey. He'd help her however he could.

And if you get the instructor position in College Station?

He would still find a way to be there for her. All the while praying that his heart remained unscathed.

Chapter Two

❧

Tori had lost almost everything she held dear. Her parents. Her husband. Now her home and everything in it. Aiden was all she had left. Her precious baby boy. How was she going to tell him they no longer had a home? That his toys, clothes and bed were gone.

Her tears spent, she drew in a shuddering breath. The strong arms that had held her tightly for who knows how long relaxed and she looked into Micah's weary face. They were both exhausted. At least he might be able to get some sleep.

Standing, she dragged her fingers through her tangled hair and looked down at Micah and Peggy. "I need to go get Aiden." She sniffed. "I don't want him to learn about this from someone else."

"I understand, dear." Her mother-in-law stood, tucking a sliver of her silver pixie-cut hair behind one ear.

"I'll drive you." Micah hauled his weary body to an upright position.

"No, Micah. You're exhausted."

"So are you." Those dark eyes bore into her. "Besides, I'd like to be there when you tell Aiden. If you don't mind."

"No, of course not." Her gaze bobbed to the floor and back before she forced a halfhearted smile. "Thank you."

After splashing some cold water on her face and gathering her hair into a messy bun, she looked down at the T-shirt and shorts she'd changed into after arriving at Peggy's yesterday. Other than her sundress, they were the only clothes she had. Thankfully, Peggy kept a few things on hand for Aiden, so he'd had something to wear to school this morning.

A knock sounded on the bathroom door.

Tori opened it to find Peggy holding a couple of folded items in her hand.

"I found some T-shirts that are way too small for me." She shrugged. "In case you'd like to change."

"You must've read my mind." She took them from her mother-in-law. "Tell Micah I'll meet him at his truck."

A few minutes later, wearing a gray United States Marines T-shirt, she joined him, feeling suddenly awkward. Holding her like a baby while she'd cried was, no doubt, pushing the boundaries of their friendship. A friendship that had seen highs and lows yet had somehow survived. It seemed, no matter what, she could always count on Micah to be there for her. He was the one who'd taken leave and come home when her mother died and when Aiden was born. Meanwhile, Joel had always been fashionably late. Swooping in unexpectedly weeks after an event.

Knowing her husband, it was probably so he wouldn't have to share the limelight. Joel had reveled in being the hero. And while he'd died that way, saving the lives of the men who were with him when they were ambushed, that was the only knowledge his son would ever have of him.

"I like your shirt." Micah grinned as she climbed into the cab of his pickup, no doubt trying to keep things upbeat.

"I thought you might."

He talked about the weather and other random things as they moved down the drive and onto the road.

"Is the fire out now?" she finally asked.

His lips pursed while his knuckles whitened atop the steering wheel. "For the most part. There are still crews out there, monitoring hot spots."

"Were other homes burned?"

"Yes. Quite a few."

She sucked in a deep breath. Let it out. "At least I'm not the only one." She looked at him. "You know what they say? Misery loves company." Though she tried to make light of things, she couldn't help wondering why God would allow such a thing to happen. Hadn't she suffered enough loss already?

All she had left was Aiden, her vehicle and memories.

"Tori?"

She looked across the center console to Micah.

"I know this seems insurmountable. But you *will* get through this. I'm willing to help you any way I can. You're a Stallings. We take care of each other."

Not all of them. Joel had left her to take care of herself. If it hadn't been for Peggy and Micah… "I appreciate that. But first things first. I have to break the news to Aiden."

She worried her bottom lip as they pulled into the parking lot of the elementary school where she worked.

They parked, got out of the vehicle and made their way to the entrance. She pressed the buzzer then identified herself to the school secretary when she responded.

By the time she and Micah walked into the office, the principal, school nurse and a couple of aides stood behind the desk. And they all wore the same worried expression.

Rubbing her arms, only in part because of the frigid air-conditioning, she said, "I'd like to pick up Aiden, please."

"Of course." Her principal nodded. "Would you like to go get him or do you want us to have him come up here?"

"Um." Her gaze drifted to Micah's.

"We can go get him," he said.

Tori nodded, thankful he was there.

They started to turn, then she realized she should let her principal know she would likely need a sub again tomorrow.

Scanning the morose faces gathered on the other side of the desk, her gaze settled on her principal's. "I, uh…" She took a deep breath. "My house burned down, so I might need a substitute tomorrow."

"Oh, sweetheart." Bethany Wilks hurried from behind the desk to envelop Tori in a hug. "I am so sorry." Setting Tori away from her, the woman continued. "You take as long as you need. We'll see to it your class is covered."

"Is there anything we can do?" Heidi Jordan, the school secretary asked.

"I-I really don't know." Tori felt Micah's strong arm come around her shoulders then.

"The news is fresh, so she's still processing," he said. "But she wanted to tell Aiden herself."

"Of course." Bethany reached for her hand. "Do you at least have a place to stay?"

Tori nodded. "Yes. At my mother-in-law's."

"Good. Glad to hear it."

Tori swallowed. "Though, I, uh… I have almost no clothes other than what I'm wearing. So I guess I'll need to come up with some things." She shrugged.

The principal arched a brow, giving her a once-over. "Size four or six?"

"Four."

"Shoe size?"

"Seven."

"And Aiden?"

"Oh. Um." After thinking for a moment—he outgrew things so fast these days—she rattled them off.

A short time later, she and Micah continued down the familiar hallway toward Aiden's classroom. She grew more nervous with each step.

"He's going to wonder why we're picking him up." She peered at the man beside her. "I don't want to worry him."

"Okay, then let's just knock on the door and when his teacher answers, you can explain things to her before she sends him out to us."

"I suppose that would work." Though it did little to settle her nerves.

Thankfully, the exchange was without issue.

"Do I have a doctor 'pointment?" her son asked before they reached the office. Obviously, he couldn't imagine any other reason for her to take him out of school before lunch.

"No, you do not." She'd tried to sound upbeat but feared she'd failed.

"Then where are we going?" He peered up at her as they neared the exit.

Outside, Micah said, "Your mom needs to tell you something, champ." Bless him for intervening. He loved her son every bit as much as she did.

"What?"

She smoothed a hand over his soft dark hair. "Let's wait 'til we're in the truck."

Micah unlocked the doors. "Aiden, why don't you join us in the front seat for a minute?"

"Okay!" The kid looked as though he'd just won a prize.

Minutes later, Tori clasped and unclasped her hands as she searched for the right words. But there was no easy way to tell her son their home and everything in it was gone. She'd just have to be as gentle as possible.

"Aiden, remember I told you why we stayed at Gigi's house last night?"

He nodded. "Cuz of the fire." He looked at his uncle then. "Did you get it put out?"

Micah's worried gaze met hers. "They're still working on it."

Aiden pondered the comment. "That must be a big fire."

"Yes, it is." Micah's voice soothed Tori's frazzled nerves.

With a bolstering breath, Tori said, "Aiden, the fire got our house."

The boy's dark eyes widened. "It burned it?"

She nodded.

Aiden faced his uncle. "How come you didn't stop it?"

Looking helpless, Micah sighed. "We tried, but the wind made the fire grow very big very fast. We had to get out of its way or it might have gotten us, too."

Aiden gasped. "That would've been bad."

"Yes, it would have been very bad," said Micah.

Aiden was quiet for a time. And while Tori wanted to know what was going on in her son's head, she kept silent, allowing him to process.

Finally, he looked her in the eye. "Where are we going to live?"

"With Gigi, for now."

The boy's face brightened. "That means I can swim in her pool every day."

Tori found herself chuckling. Leave it to a child to look at the bright side. "Weather permitting, I suppose you can do that."

Suddenly, his eyes widened. "Oh, no! My toys!" The panic in his voice had Tori's chest squeezing. Tears sprang to her eyes and she blinked at a frenzied pace to keep them from falling. She did not want to cry in front of her son.

"I'm sorry, Aiden." Micah turned the boy to face him. "The fire consumed everything. But stuff like toys and clothes can be replaced. You and your mama? Well, you're irreplaceable. We need to thank God the two of you are safe."

While Tori knew Micah was right, she didn't feel like thanking God right now. After all, He'd allowed this to happen to them. Yes, she was grateful she and Aiden were safe, but hadn't she lost enough already? Now they were left with only the clothes on their backs.

All these years, through each loss, she'd done her best to remain positive, clinging to God's promise that all things worked together for good.

A lot of good that had done her.

"Can I go back to my classroom now?"

Tori looked at her son, wondering if she'd heard him right. "You want to go back to school?"

"Uh-huh." He nodded. "I don't want to miss recess and playing with my friends."

"Oh." Tori was stupefied. She thought for sure he'd want to go back to Peggy's. "I-I guess that's okay. You're sure?"

More nodding.

"Let's get you back inside then."

"Okay, Mama."

As they returned to the school, Tori decided him staying might be a good thing after all. Because, while she had a strong desire to see what remained of her house, she couldn't do that to Aiden. At least, not until she'd had an opportunity to see it first. If things were as bad as Micah had said, she'd be in no shape to console her son.

Micah waited in the truck while Tori walked Aiden back to his classroom, thankful things had gone relatively smoothly with the boy. Then again, Micah knew all too well how grief was sometimes delayed and could very well sneak up on his nephew hours, days, even weeks, later. He'd be sure to keep a watchful eye on the kid.

For now, though, with Aiden remaining at school, Micah could head home and get some much-needed shut-eye. He dragged a hand over his face as weariness seeped into his bones. As long as he could get in a few solid hours of sleep before Aiden got home from school, he should be good to go until bedtime.

At the sound of the passenger door opening, he turned as Tori climbed into the cab. "I certainly hadn't expected that." She pulled the door closed before reaching for her seat belt. "Do you think he has any comprehension of what happened?"

"No." Neither did Tori. The images people saw on television never revealed the full magnitude of a situation. "We'll want to monitor his behavior. Anger and disobedience are common manifestations of grief, especially in kids. They aren't equipped to handle tragedy." He puffed out a laugh. "None of us are. But Aiden doesn't have the maturity to understand things the way we do." Shifting the truck into gear, he added, "We'll just need to make sure we're there for him if or when he hits that brick wall."

"I guess I'll have to take your word for it. You've been witness to a lot more fires than I have."

He eased off the brake and started out of the parking space. "I'm not sure if that's a good thing or not, but yes, I have." Maneuvering past the rows of vehicles, he aimed for the exit.

Tori stared straight ahead. "I think I'm going to drive out to my house and check out the damage."

Micah slammed on the brake. "You want to go see your house *now*?" He couldn't help the incredulity in his voice as he glared at Tori.

She nodded. "Don't worry. You don't have to go. I'll take my vehicle." Meeting his gaze, she added, "That way, you can sleep."

As if thoughts of her trekking around the pile of ashes that was now her home would allow him to sleep. Tori had no idea what she was in for, mentally or otherwise. The land surrounding her house had been hit by the hottest part of the fire. The dense woods that had once spread across the area now looked almost apocalyptic with trees resembling charred matchsticks stretching up from the ash-covered ground.

"There's no way I'm going to let you go out there alone."

"Micah, you're exhausted."

"And you're not?" From what his mother had said, Tori hadn't gotten any sleep either.

Shaking his head, he again moved toward the exit. "I don't even know if they'll let anyone in yet. There are still hot spots." He sighed, rubbing the scruff coating his chin. "Though I suppose this would be a good time since Aiden decided to stay at school."

"Exactly!" Her emphatic nod had the blond hair piled atop her head wobbling.

Easing onto the street, he said, "I will take you on one condition."

"Which is?"

"You do what I say, and if they refuse to let us in, you don't argue."

"That's two things."

He glared across the cab. "Don't try me, Tori."

She flopped back against her seat and crossed her arms. "Sorry. I'm a little punchy."

"And I'm getting grumpy, so I guess we make a good pair."

"Have you eaten anything?" she asked.

"I had a couple of breakfast tacos a few hours ago. But I could use some coffee. How about you?"

"I definitely need coffee. I'm not hungry, though."

"When was the last time you ate anything?"

"Lunch yesterday," he heard her say under her breath.

"In that case, I'm pulling into Plowman's so we can grab something." Hope Crossing would be lost without their one-stop feed store that carried everything from fresh-baked goods to hardware and horse saddles.

Thankfully, he'd managed to talk Tori into a breakfast taco while he'd ordered half a dozen pumpkin kolaches. What could he say? He was a pumpkin-spice guy through and through. Though he'd probably end up sharing with Tori since they were her favorite, too.

Back in his truck, they headed west of town on the farm-to-market road. All the while, Tori's phone kept making all sorts of noises.

"Are you playing some game over there?"

"No. Everybody and his brother is texting me." Her ringtone sounded then. "Oh, good grief." She sent him an exasperated look. "I don't have time for all of this."

"Turn it off then."

"What if the school calls?"

"They have Mom's and my number. And since we're together…" He lifted a shoulder.

"Okay." She sighed. "Done."

Nearing her road, Micah noticed the blockade was gone, so he made the turn.

Continuing along the narrow, paved road flanked by pastures that looked the same today as they had yesterday, no one would guess a wildfire had threatened them less than twenty-four hours ago. A mile up the road, however, it was a different story. And Micah couldn't help wondering how Tori would react when she laid eyes on the devastation.

He hesitated, easing his foot off the gas pedal as he approached the burned-out area. "You're sure you want to do this?"

"Yes. I mean I'm going to have to eventually. May as well git 'er done, right?" She sounded as though she was trying to convince herself.

Easing to the side of the road, he brought the truck to a stop before facing her. "Tori, if you're having second thoughts, we can go back to Mom's. Just say the word."

She drew in a long breath. Stared at her clasped hands. "Honestly, I don't know how I'm going to react. Yeah, I'm scared. But the not knowing is worse. At least once I see it, no matter how bad things are, I can begin moving forward. I hope so, anyway." Her blue eyes met his. "Right now there's a whole lot of uncertainty weighing on me."

He nodded. "I can appreciate that." After a deep breath, he added, "Let's do this then." With that, he eased back onto the road.

Moments later, a blackened pasture, still surrounded by its barbed-wire fence, was the first visible sign that a fire had ravaged the area.

"While the fire jumped the road—" he pointed to the wooded area on their left "—it wasn't near as intense on the other side."

"How come?"

"In part, because of the road. And the forest service cut firebreaks through the woods with bulldozers. However, there's also a lot of yaupon growing among the trees over there and, unlike the pines, yaupon doesn't burn easily and actually helped to slow down the fire."

"Really? And I always thought yaupons were bad."

"Guess it depends on your perspective." He eased around a curve, knowing the bulk of the devastation lay on the other side of it.

Then he heard Tori's gasp.

"Oh, my." She touched her long, slender fingers to her lips. "This looks *so* different." She glanced his way. "We could never see through the woods before. It was too thick."

"The underbrush was burned up."

"How come some trees still have leaves while others are barren?"

He sighed. "When it comes to fire, there's no rhyme or reason."

"Looks like the Parsons' house is gone." Tori stared out the window, her tone somber as they passed what had been a single-story ranchette. Now it was nothing more than ashes.

"This is the area that was hit the hardest." He continued past another drive. The house there had been set a good ways back from the road. Though that hadn't spared it from the flames.

Next up was Tori's house, and her face was all but pressed to the window.

He moved slowly, inching past the once heavily wooded area that had been reduced to bare-bones trees. Through the charred trunks, he could see where Tori's house had once sat. But if she'd seen it, she had yet to say anything.

Approaching the driveway, he watched her. Saw her shoulders fall. "How are you doing over there?"

"I think I'm numb." She twisted to face him. "It feels like I'm in a dream."

If only that were true. Sadly, it was all too real.

He barely eased into the drive. "I want to check things out before I go any farther. Make sure it's safe."

"That's okay." She reached for her door. "I can walk from here."

Not without him, she wasn't.

He killed the engine, opened the door, tossing it closed before hurrying to join her. "You'll want to watch where you step." Only then did he realize she was wearing flip-flops. "Hold up. You can't go walking around in those." He pointed to her footwear before starting to the back of his truck where he retrieved a pair of rubber boots he kept tucked upside down in the gap between the cab and bed. "Put these on, please. They may be big, but they'll protect your feet."

"Thank you." She promptly made the switch then tossed her own footwear in the cab.

The smell of smoke enveloped them as they continued along the dirt drive.

Pausing just short of where the gate had been on the charming picket fence that had encircled the three-bedroom, two-bath house, Tori wrapped her arms around her middle.

While the brick fireplace stood sentry to their left, smoke still wafted from the ash heap that had once been her home. For more than a century, the beautiful Victorian with its elaborate trim had faced its share of nature's wrath. Ice storms, flooding rains, blistering summers. But the grand dame hadn't stood a chance against yesterday's inferno.

Looking from the devastation to Tori, he noticed she was shaking. Her face contorted as tears spilled onto her cheeks.

"Tori?" When he set an arm around her shoulders, she turned into him, sobbing.

He held her close, letting her cry, whispering words meant to soothe though likely not helping at all. Tori was more than his sister-in-law, she was his friend. And while his brother had routinely left Tori alone to handle whatever life had thrown her way, Micah couldn't bring himself to do that. Not now. Not ever.

As sorrow continued to rack her body, Micah ached for his friend. Longed to take away her pain. Yet, for as much as it aggrieved him to see her like this, he also knew it marked the beginning of the healing process. A process that could take months. Even years.

But she wouldn't have to do it alone. No matter how uncomfortable it might make him, Micah would do whatever it took to see Tori and Aiden happy again.

Chapter Three

Tori stared out the windshield, silent as Micah drove back to his mother's place, still trying to grasp the reality that her beautiful home was gone. The place that had been her shelter from so many of life's storms. The one constant in her life, destroyed by an act of God.

Why? Why would God do that to her now when she'd finally started making it their own? He'd already taken her parents and her husband. How much more would He rip from her hands?

Trust in the Lord with all thine heart; and lean not unto thine own understanding.

She scoffed. A lot of good that had done her.

A brief glance toward the driver's seat had her wondering what she would've done if Micah hadn't been with her. She'd known the situation was going to be bad, but the utter devastation had been beyond her imagination. Yet Micah had held her while she'd blubbered all over him, mourning another loss. Seemed he'd always been her rock in times of trouble.

She eyed the dark-haired man in the driver's seat who was too tenderhearted to let her face this disaster alone, thankful he hadn't. But she'd taken up enough of his time. He needed to rest.

Returning her gaze to the road, she caught a whiff of the smoky aroma emanating from her clothes, taunting her as she looked out over the countryside. The nauseating smell seemed to surround her.

And to think, she'd always loved the smell of a campfire.

She glimpsed the clock on the dash. One forty-five? How could that be? If she hurried, she'd have just enough time to shower before going to pick up Aiden.

Then she remembered she had no clean clothes, other than the remaining T-shirts Peggy had given her this morning. Even so, her shorts reeked. Her only other option was the sundress she'd worn yesterday. She supposed that would have to do.

Micah cleared his throat. "I'd say 'penny for your thoughts,' but I have a feeling you've got so many running through your head that it would cost me a small fortune."

"Pretty much." Glancing across the center console, she caught him yawning.

That made her yawn. Something she couldn't afford right now. Not with school dismissing soon. She wanted—needed—to be with her son. Now that he'd had time to process the news she'd given him this morning, Aiden might have questions or need assurance that they were safe. That they'd, somehow, start over. And for that, she needed her wits about her.

Another pot of coffee was definitely in order.

"Look, Tori." Micah interrupted her thoughts. "I know things seem overwhelming right now."

"You think?"

Eyes on the road, he frowned. "You're snarky when you're tired."

"And you're just now figuring that out?"

"More like stating the obvious." He scowled. "What I

was *going* to say is that it's gonna take time for you to sort through everything. Your emotions, insurance, your future. It's a process, so don't feel rushed. You and Aiden have a home at Mom's for as long as you need, so give yourself a little grace while you contemplate how to proceed."

"At the moment, I'd be contented with some clean clothes."

His lopsided smile held an air of mischief. "I might still have a pair of jogging pants and a Brooks and Dunn T-shirt from high school that would probably fit you."

She swatted the man who'd once been on the scrawny side, wondering when his biceps had gotten so huge. "Very funny, Stallings."

When the laughter subsided, he said, "Seriously, Tori. You're not alone. Mom and I are your family and we're here for you and Aiden. I'll do whatever takes to help you bounce back from this."

Humbled, she stared at her clasped hands in her lap. "You've always been there for me, Micah." For all the highs and lows in her life. Even when Joel hadn't been. "I appreciate that more than words can express." Micah was one of the good guys. If he were in an old Western movie, he'd be the guy riding in on a white horse to save the day. Why some woman hadn't taken him off the market years ago was beyond her.

"We're blessed to serve a God who promises to provide everything we need. Like Paul said in Philippians, '…my God shall supply all your need according to his riches in glory by Christ Jesus.'"

Tori bit back a snide remark. God hadn't supplied much for her. Instead, He kept taking.

Hoping to change the subject, she said, "Speaking of needs, after I grab Aiden, I think we'll go on over to Brenham. We both need clothes, toiletries, and who knows how many other things."

"Want me to go—"

"No!" Her palm shot up. "I've taken up enough of your time. You need to sleep. And that will be much easier to do with Aiden out of the house."

Approaching his mother's, Tori noticed Hank's truck in the drive. "Looks like your mom has company."

"Yeah." Micah grinned. "Seems she and Hank can't stand to be apart for too long. I think things might be getting serious between them."

"I don't think that's such a bad thing." Peggy had been widowed for almost a decade and she was still relatively young. She deserved to love and be loved. Actually, Tori was rather envious of the woman. Having someone who cared about her and who sought to meet her needs.

Tori's gaze drifted to Micah. If he weren't her brother-in-law. She quickly looked away.

"No, it's not. Hank's a good man," said Micah. "And he makes Mama smile." He paused then. "I am a little surprised, though."

"About what?"

"That there aren't more people here."

"Why do you say that?"

"Oh, come on." Micah cast her a glance. "You know how the people of Hope Crossing are. They take care of their own. Once word gets out about your house, the cavalry will be headed your way."

In droves, as Tori recalled. That was one of the reasons she'd moved back here so many years ago. Though she and Joel had lived in military housing at Camp Lejeune, he'd been deployed most of the time, leaving her alone more often than not. So when her mother had gotten sick, Tori had returned to Hope Crossing to care for her. Then, after Mom had passed and the whole town rallied around Tori, she hadn't been able to bring herself to leave again.

Micah parked and they stepped out of the truck into the sticky afternoon heat.

"Thank you, Micah, for accompanying me today. I know you're exhausted and would much rather be sleeping, but once again, you were my rock."

He shrugged. "Friends take care of each other."

"Yes, but none better than you." Then, before she could think better of it, she wrapped her arms around his waist and hugged him, willing even a morsel of his fortitude to seep into her. "Sorry, I know I smell." Her cheeks heated when she released him.

"Hey, at least we're wearing the same scent." He winked and nodded in the direction of the house. "C'mon." Moments later, he opened the kitchen door, allowing her to enter the space with golden-oak cabinetry and pale gray tile floors first.

"There you are." A smiling Peggy stood on the other side of the granite-topped peninsula with Hank, munching on something.

"How's it going?" Micah nodded. "Hey, Hank."

Glancing at the oak table surrounded by matching Windsor chairs to her left, Tori found it covered with bags and storage containers. "What's all this?"

"Gloriana stopped by," said Peggy.

Gloriana had been one of Tori's best friends since they were kids and Tori had served as matron of honor when Gloriana married almost two years ago.

"I called her after you left this morning to let her know what had happened." Peggy moved around the counter to join them. "Naturally, she wanted to help. So, after I let her know what sizes Aiden wore, she went shopping. Dropped all of this off about thirty minutes ago, along with some food from her mother."

"Francie sent food?" Micah brightened. Francie Krenek—formerly Francie Prescott—was one of Hope Crossing's best cooks.

Peggy nodded. "Fried chicken, mashed potatoes, corn, green beans and some delectable cookies and cream brownies Hank and I were just sampling."

"Mmm, mmm." Micah rubbed his flat stomach. "I'm ready to dig in right now."

"You may as well." His mother waved a hand toward the stovetop. "I'm sure there'll be plenty more food coming our way. People have been calling all day, wanting to know how they can help. Evidently they couldn't get through to you, Tori."

"Sorry. My phone started blowing up, so I turned it off."

"I don't blame you. People mean well, but they can be overwhelming." Slipping an arm around Tori's shoulder, Peggy turned her attention back to the table. "Gloriana must've shopped all morning. Said she got anything she'd be missing if she were in your position. Shoes and clothes for both you and Aiden, along with undergarments, toiletries, makeup. And she left all of the receipts in case you need to return or exchange anything."

Tears blurred Tori's vision. "That was so thoughtful of her. I was planning to take Aiden shopping after school." She glanced at her mother-in-law. "Guess there's no need now." Tentatively peering into the bags, she said, "I need to call and thank her." She lifted the lid on one of the clear bins to discover her favorite body wash, shampoo and conditioner. Even a bath pouf, brush and comb, blow dryer and straightener. "She really did think of everything."

Digging into the first big bag, she discovered multiple outfits and casual dresses that would be perfect for school. Even a lightweight cardigan that would come in handy in her perpetually cold classroom. The next bag contained everyday wear like T-shirts, shorts and jeans, while a glimpse of the others revealed an ample array of clothing for Aiden.

Gloriana had really outdone herself.

Realizing she didn't have time to go through everything, Tori snagged a pair of shorts and a plain black tee before grabbing the storage container brimming with toiletries and scurrying upstairs to the bedroom she'd be using for the foreseeable future for a shower.

Twenty minutes later, she emerged feeling somewhat revived, not to mention eager to see her son.

Since Micah was nowhere to be found, Tori assumed he'd gone to bed, so she let Peggy know she was leaving before heading out the door.

The back of her vehicle still held the items she'd rescued from her house yesterday. She supposed she'd better get them inside and out of the heat. Especially the photos.

Task completed, she drove to the elementary school where she eased into the pickup line to wait. Retrieving her phone from her purse, she turned it on. Moments later, the device beeped, pinged and buzzed, alerting her of missed calls, voicemails and texts. Noting that kids were emerging from the school, she shot off a quick text of thanks to Gloriana and then turned the device off again. She didn't want anything or anyone interrupting her time with Aiden.

Reaching the front of the line, Tori watched as the aide opened the back door on the passenger side.

"Here you go, Aiden." Erica Morris waved him to her. "Did you forget your backpack?"

Tori's heart dipped. She hadn't thought to grab his backpack from the house yesterday.

"I don't have one." He peered up at the woman with the same dark eyes as his father and uncle. "It got burned in the fire."

The woman's mouth made an *O* as she dipped to glance inside the vehicle to Tori. "I heard. I'm so sorry."

"Thank you, Erica." Tori motioned for Aiden. "Come on, little man."

Erica closed the door and Tori pulled away, forcing what she hoped was a normal smile.

"How was the rest of your day?" She glanced back at Aiden to find him staring out the window.

"Okay. Jeremy and Trevor said they'd give me some of their toys." Brady's twins were so sweet. "And then Maddy Walker hugged me in front of *everyone*."

Tori couldn't help smiling. That sounded like something Jake and Alli's little girl would do. "She was only trying to make you feel better."

"Girl hugs are icky."

"Gigi and I hug you all the time." In the rearview mirror, she saw him look her way.

"But you're not girls. I like your hugs."

Easing out of the parking lot, she said, "That's good, because your hugs are the best thing ever."

"Can I go swimming when we get to Gigi's?"

"Do you have any homework?"

"No."

"Then yes you may." She increased her speed at the end of the school zone.

"Can Uncle Micah swim with me? I like it when he swims with me."

"Your uncle is probably asleep." At least, she hoped so. "He was up all night, fighting that fire. That's hard work."

"How come he let the fire get to our house? Firemen are s'posed to put the fire out."

Her grip on the steering wheel tightened. "Remember what Micah said. They tried, but the fire was too big, and moving very fast."

"So he coulda got hurt?"

"Yes, he could have."

He thought for a moment. "I'm glad he didn't get hurt, cuz then he wouldn't be able to play with me."

"That's right."

"Maybe you could swim with me."

Considering all she wanted was to be with her son… "I'd like that very much." Thankfully, she kept a swimsuit at Peggy's for such occasions.

When they neared the Stallings' home a short time later, there were numerous vehicles in the driveway.

She sighed. While she appreciated the community's eagerness to help, she was not in the mood to rehash what had happened over and over again.

"Is Gigi having a party?" Aiden asked as they pulled into the drive.

"No, sweetie. I think they're here to see you and me, and to bring us things."

"What kinds of things?"

"Food. Clothes. They want to help replace things we lost in the fire."

"Toys?"

She shrugged. "Possibly, but I wouldn't count on it." While she'd decided against going shopping today, she made a mental note to get a new backpack as well as some toys.

When they entered the kitchen a short time later, several women from the church looked their way. And before she could say hello, they'd surrounded her, taking turns hugging her and telling her what they'd brought. As if she'd remember.

"We're praying for you," one woman said. "Remember, God won't give us more than we can handle."

"God love you, doll." Dottie Rodgers, Tori's old Sunday school teacher, embraced her, smoothing a hand over her back. "You've been through so much already."

The next woman patted Tori's hand. "I know things seem bleak, but God is good. *All* the time."

As Tori's blood began to boil, she closed her eyes. Nonetheless, her breaths came faster. If she heard one more platitude…

"Honey—" Glenda Wasserman, a former teacher at the elementary school, wagged a finger in Tori's direction, her expression stern "—just remember, God's got this, and you, in the palm of His hand."

Nostrils flaring, Tori covered her ears. *"Stop it!"* She looked from one shocked face to the next. "God is *not* good. He's turned His back on me time and time again. So y'all can believe what you want, but if this is God's best for me, then I'm done with Him." Eager to escape, she turned, only to find a frowning Micah standing on the other side of the counter. And he was holding a crying Aiden.

Micah wasn't near as surprised by Tori's outburst yesterday as he'd have thought. The woman had been distraught and was running on fumes. The last thing she'd needed was to find herself overwhelmed by a bunch of visitors, no matter how good their intentions might have been.

Now, as he locked the door to his classroom at Brenham High School a little before four-thirty Tuesday, he was still kicking himself for not intervening on her behalf. Instead, he'd just stood there watching her inch toward the edge of a proverbial cliff and done nothing to prevent her from falling. Sure, Aiden had been disturbed, seeing his mother so agitated, but Micah could've passed him off to his grandmother. Instead, he'd let Tori topple over the brink.

He slung his backpack over one shoulder, determined steps propelling him down the polished hallway, through the metal door, into the afternoon heat and across the parking lot. Since his earlier texts had gone unanswered, along with his lunchtime phone call, he wondered if Tori had again turned off her phone. Either that or she was ignoring him. Whatever the circumstances, he was eager to know how she was doing.

Tossing his pack into the cab first, he climbed into the truck, started the engine and hastily made his way out of the parking lot as hot air spewed from the vents. He prayed a good night's rest had improved Tori's outlook. At least, he hoped she'd slept well. Despite his own nagging concerns, he'd crashed as soon as his head had hit the pillow. Then he'd left the house this morning before she and Aiden were up.

With the sun blazing overhead, he continued from Brenham into the countryside, the truck cab finally cool. He eyed a small herd of Charolais seeking shade beneath a large oak tree, thoughts of his nephew prodding his heart. The poor kid had sought him out yesterday after walking into the house with his mother and seeing all those women. Micah knew the ladies had meant well, but they'd seemed to have no clue how daunting they were. After all Tori had been through, it was no wonder she'd snapped.

God is not good. He's turned His back on me time and time again.

The words had shocked him every bit as much as the

women they'd been directed at. Tori couldn't have meant them, though. She'd always held tight to her faith. She was simply at her wits end from sleep deprivation and all the stress of the previous twenty-four hours. Perhaps she'd hoped to jolt the women into leaving. There's no way she'd meant what she'd said. Though, if she had, there were problems even bigger than her house being destroyed that needed to be addressed.

Approaching the farm, he glimpsed his mother's vehicle in the driveway, but Tori's was gone. Hmm. Maybe she'd taken Aiden shopping. She'd mentioned getting him some toys.

After parking, he grabbed his pack and went into the house, where he found his mother standing in front of the open refrigerator, holding a foil-covered pan.

"What's going on?" He dropped his things in one of the chairs around the table.

"Oh, just moving some of this food to the deep freeze." Holding one pan, she nodded at two more on the counter.

"Where's Tori?"

Mom bumped the refrigerator door closed with her elbow. "Aiden wanted to see their house, so she took him over there."

"What?" Why hadn't Tori waited for him? He would've gone with them.

He sighed, recognizing he had no right to be upset. Aiden wasn't his son. Still, he wanted to be there for his nephew's physical and mental wellbeing. Besides, there could still be hot spots lurking in the ashes. And there was no telling the potential dangers scattered about that could pose a threat to a curious little boy.

"How long ago did they leave?"

His mother thought a moment. "Maybe thirty minutes."

"I'm going over there." He returned to the door. "If they get back before I do, let me know, please."

Throwing himself back into his pickup, he raced out of the drive, recalling Tori's reaction to seeing her home yesterday. Did she have the fortitude to hold herself together today? He should have asked his mother how Tori was doing, because the only thing worse than Aiden having a negative reaction would be both of them having a meltdown.

Micah sucked in a breath as he continued through town and toward Tori's. *Lord, please protect them, both physically and emotionally. I know this event has been a huge blow to their lives, but I also know that You have them in the palm of Your mighty hand. Guide my words and help me not to react negatively. Amen.*

A short time later, he rolled down Tori's road, taking in the countryside, particularly when he reached the burn area. According to a text he'd received from the chief, they still had a small crew monitoring the area, but there had been nothing of concern. Just a few minor hot spots. Nothing near Tori's, though.

He spotted her vehicle up ahead, barely in her drive, the way he'd done yesterday. So he eased onto the shoulder and came to a stop this side of it.

The sun filtered through scorched trees. And he could see Aiden and Tori walking around.

Micah exited his truck, tossing the door closed behind him.

The sound had Aiden looking his way. "Uncle Micah!"

As the kid broke into a jog, Micah noticed he was wearing rubber boots.

Micah picked up his pace, his long strides erasing the space in no time. And when he stooped, the kid launched himself into Micah's arms.

"How's it going? How was school?"

"Good. Jeremy and Trevor brought me a new backpack."

"That was nice of them."

Aiden nodded. "It even had some dinosaurs and a dinosaur shirt inside."

"Wow! Sounds like you've got some really great friends." He lifted one of the kid's booted feet. "Where'd you get these?"

"Mama got both of us some. She said I couldn't walk out here without them."

"That mother of yours is a smart cookie." He glanced at Tori, who stood opposite him in what had been their backyard, clad in skinny jeans and a T-shirt.

The boy squirmed out of Micah's arms. "Come see something."

He followed his nephew around what had been their house, past the old chimney to a smaller pile of charred wood and melted plastic.

"The fire burned my swing set." Aiden pointed to the deformed slide.

Micah had built the wooden playset for the kid's birthday two years ago. And Aiden played on it all the time.

His nephew peered up at him with sad eyes. "Will you build me a new one?"

"I sure will, buddy."

A smile lit the boy's face. "Really?"

"You betcha."

A few feet away, amid the aroma of charred wood, Tori had yet to say a word. Instead, she seemed to wander aimlessly, occasionally pausing to pick up something then examine it before tossing it aside.

Micah inched toward her. "How's it going?"

"It's going." She barely looked at him.

"How'd you sleep last night?"

She kept her eyes focused on the ground. "Okay, I guess. Once I finally fell asleep, I didn't wake up until my alarm went off."

Hands tucked in the pockets of his jeans, he said, "I tried calling you. I'm guessing you turned your phone off again. Or were you avoiding me?"

The corners of her mouth lifted a notch as she met his gaze. "I'd never avoid you. But I did turn it off."

"That's good to know." He continued to watch her. "What did you do today?"

With a deep breath, she said, "I spoke with my insurance agent this morning. He's going to come out here tomorrow. In the meantime, I'm supposed to start making a list of everything that was in my house." She toed the ground with her rubber boot. "Don't know how I'm supposed to do that when it's all gone."

"I'll help you. We'll mentally walk through every room. Open every door and drawer."

She rolled those blue eyes that had yet to meet his. "Sounds exhausting."

"Bite-size pieces, Tori. We don't have to do it all at once."

Lips pursed, she nodded.

He visually located Aiden, who appeared to be drawing in the ash with a stick. "So, according to Mom, there's been more food coming in."

"Along with donations of money, clothing, gift cards."

"People are generous. They see a need and they want to help the best way they know how."

Again, she nodded.

"Look—" he touched her elbow "—we all understand you were overwhelmed yesterday. And probably still are today."

"Yes, to both. But I know where you're going with this." Crossing her arms, she looked at him. "I meant what I said to those women yesterday. I'm done trusting a god who has taken everything from me."

"Not everything. You still have Aiden." He again glanced at the boy, tempted to bring up Job from the Bible. He'd not only lost his home, but his livelihood and his children. But this wasn't the time for that. Tori was too combative, which was rather interesting for the usually happy-go-lucky, always-ready-with-a-smile woman.

"You know…" He returned his attention to Tori. "Just because we're Christians doesn't mean we're going to have a problem-free life."

"Maybe not, but I can't seem to catch a break." She raised her head, her chin jutting out. "I begged God to heal Mom. I prayed for Joel's safety. I asked Him to spare my house."

"So, you're giving up on Him because He didn't do things the way you wanted?"

She glared at him.

"Tori, your mom was ready to go Home. Joel chose to return overseas."

"Are you saying they wanted to leave me?"

"You're twisting my words."

She turned away from him. "I don't want to talk about this. I have a home to rebuild."

"Is that what you've decided to do?" Pretty quick if you asked him. Then again, this early in the process, she might change her mind a thousand times.

Glancing over her shoulder, she said, "Rebuild in the generic sense. I haven't thought that far ahead."

"Can we go now?"

Micah turned to see Aiden coming toward them.

"I'm hot," the kid continued. "I wanna go swimming."

Starting for her son, Tori said, "Yes, we can go back to Gigi's. Supper should be arriving soon." She looked at Micah. "Don't worry, I'll be on my best behavior."

As they started toward their vehicles, Aiden said, "Can I ride with Uncle Micah?"

"That's up to him," said Tori.

"Of course, you can." Micah ruffled the kid's dark hair. "Come on."

Once Aiden was buckled into the booster seat Micah kept in his truck, Micah made a U-turn and started up the road.

Moments into their journey, Aiden spoke from the back seat. "Why is Mama mad at God? It's not God's fault our house burned down. He didn't do it. The fire did."

Uncertain of how to respond, Micah eyed him in the rearview mirror. "How do you feel about the fire?"

"I don't like that it burned all my stuff. Or that Mama is sad and mad. But I like that I have a pool now. And that I get to live with you."

Micah liked that part, too. The only problem was it also meant spending more time with Tori. Something he'd been able to manage when she'd had her own home. Now, he'd see her multiple times throughout each and every day. Work side by side with her on her fire claim. Share meals. Enjoy her company. Smell her sweet fragrance.

"I know you're my uncle, but I wish you were my dad," Aiden added. "Now that we live in the same house and get to see each other all the time, it'll be kinda like you're my dad."

Aiden's words carved a quick path to Micah's heart, wrapping around it and refusing to let go. Micah couldn't think of any greater honor. He loved Aiden like a son. But Micah was his uncle. A fact he'd do well to remember.

Because one day Tori would fall in love again and marry someone Micah hoped would love Aiden as his own. Then Micah would fade into the background once again, ignoring his true feelings for Tori, just the way he'd done when Joel had married her.

Chapter Four

The tentacles of uncertainty taunted Tori. And she wasn't a fan.

While Aiden splashed around the pool in Peggy's backyard Sunday afternoon, Tori sat at the umbrellaed table nearby, waggling the pen tucked between her middle and index fingers as she stared at the blank yellow legal pad. For, perhaps, the first time in her life, she didn't have a plan. Not one clue as to how to move on. Life as she'd known it had come to an end and she was back to square one.

She puffed out a cynical laugh. Nope. Square one was gone, too. That beautiful Victorian had been the one constant in her life. Through good times and bad, the old dame had been her haven through all of life's storms. Now it was gone and Tori had no idea how to begin rebuilding the life she and Aiden had come to know. Where would she even start?

According to her insurance agent, she had enough coverage to do almost anything she wanted, whether it was to build new or buy existing. He'd even cut her a hefty check when he'd visited on Wednesday to cover immediate necessities and expenses. The easy stuff. She could handle the day-to-day. But what about their future?

"Mama, watch."

Her gaze drifted to the pool where her son bobbed up and

down in the shallow end, his blue goggles making him look like a bug. She watched as he dove underwater, thrashing his legs before managing a momentary handstand. Seconds later, his head broke through the surface, his grin wide.

"Good job, Aiden." She applauded. "You've been practicing very hard, and all that practice is paying off." Not to mention wearing him out. The kid had slept like a rock every night this week.

Too bad she couldn't say the same for herself. But lying in the dark, surrounded by stillness, only seemed to set her mind to racing.

"Are you ready to get out?"

Swiping his dark hair away from his face, he shook his head. "When will Uncle Micah be back?"

"I don't know. He's doing some work at the fire station."

"Oh." He thought for a moment. "Can you take a video of me and send it to him?" Her boy sure adored his uncle. But then, Micah was the only father figure Aiden had ever had in his life.

Retrieving her phone from the table, she tapped the screen to open her camera. After switching it to video mode, she stood and moved closer to the water. "I'm ready when you are."

She tapped the icon as Aiden kicked and splashed his way into another successful handstand, continuing until he emerged once again. "Excellent!" After thumbing a couple of buttons, she said, "Okay, I sent it to him."

"Yes!" Bobbing back and forth, Aiden thrust a fist into the air.

She slid the device into the back pocket of the denim shorts she'd bought on one of her big shopping trips Thursday and Friday. Buying clothes had never been so exhausting. "Now, are you ready to get out?"

"No."

"All right. Just let me know when you're done." She returned to the table, sweat trickling down her back as she wondered what it would be like to be that carefree.

Easing into her seat, Tori felt as though the weight of the world was on her shoulders. That house had held so many memories. She couldn't even imagine living somewhere else.

Then again, even if she were to build the exact same house in the same spot, things would still be different. The fire had seen to that. While most of the charred trees remained standing, they would soon die, forever changing the beautiful wooded landscape she'd known since childhood.

Her phone beeped and she looked at the screen to see a response from Micah.

That is one happy kid. Not to mention determined.

No doubt about that. Micah had been working to help Aiden master the feat all summer.

Her thumbs moved across the screen.

He had a good teacher.

Micah had the patience of Job when it came to Aiden. Her, too, now that she thought about it.

Though the message showed as Read, there was no further response.

Just as well. She'd never get anywhere if she kept getting distracted.

"Well, look at you. *Lounging* by the pool."

Tori looked up to find Gloriana strolling toward her, wearing a cute denim sundress that stopped at her knees.

"Hey." Tori stood to hug her friend, savoring the warm embrace. "How are you feeling?" Gloriana had recently told her she and Justin were expecting their third child.

"Surprisingly well." With a final squeeze, Gloriana took a step back, capturing Tori's hands in the process. "Sorry I haven't been able to get by sooner. This has been a crazy week."

"No apologies necessary. After all that stuff you brought by Monday. You must've spent hours shopping."

The dark-haired beauty waved a hand. "That was a mission I was intent on completing. I couldn't fathom waking up to learn that everything I had was gone. And since I know your tastes…" She shrugged. "It was easy."

"I don't think I'll ever find the words to tell you how much that meant to me. Coming home to find those things was a bright light in a very dark day."

"Ms. Gloriana?"

They both turned their attention to the pool where a grinning Aiden said, "Look what I can do."

After a couple of false starts, he finally managed to get both feet into the air.

"That's very impressive, Aiden," Gloriana said when he emerged from the water.

He beamed with pride. "I know."

The two women chuckled.

Looping her arm through her friend's, Tori started for the table.

"He's getting so big," said Gloriana. "Doesn't he have a birthday coming up?"

Tori gasped, her palm making contact with her forehead. "I almost forgot!"

Gloriana stopped beside the table, her brow puckering. "What?"

"His invitations. I bought some the other day, but I still need to get them out. His party is two weeks from yesterday."

"Can you pass them out at school tomorrow? Assuming you're returning to work."

"I am. And yes, since he's inviting his whole class. I forgot all about them, though. I could've been getting them ready while I sat out here." Instead of focusing on Aiden, she'd been consumed with her own problems.

"Sweetie, it's not like you don't have other things on your mind." Gloriana eased into the chair opposite the one Tori had vacated. "That reminds me, how did things go yesterday? I hate that I couldn't be there to help, but Kyleigh had a competition in Essexville." Gloriana's daughter was a barrel racer and county fairs all across the area were hosting rodeos almost every weekend this time of year.

"No worries." Tori took her own seat. "Honestly, it was kind of surreal. I mean a three-bedroom, two-bath house reduced to not much more than a foot of ash." She shook her head, thinking about the dozen friends that had joined her, Micah, Peggy and Hank to help sift through the remains to see if anything of value could be found.

"Mama said they actually unearthed a few items." Gloriana leaned back in her chair.

"Yeah. I was surprised. Mostly stuff that had been in the attic. A collection of padlocks with keys, vintage glass soda bottles that had melted, even a virtually unscathed set of china."

"That's amazing."

"Thanks to Francie—" Gloriana's mama "—everyone was well fed. Though I suspect that may have been why so many people showed up."

"I know Hawkins and Annalise —" Gloriana's brother and sister-in-law "—were planning to come."

Tori nodded. "They were there with Olivia and baby Duke, along with Brady, Kirsten and the twins. Gabriel, Jillian and Noel popped by, too, as did Jake and Alli Walker and their three kiddos. Having all those kids there kept Aiden entertained."

"I'm thankful you had so much help. One less thing for you to worry about."

Tori attempted a slight smile. "I suppose." If only she could figure out where to go from here.

"We missed you at church today."

Tori set to work gathering the items she had strewn across the table into a neat pile. "I had a headache." Though it wasn't a lie, it was still the lamest excuse in the book. Not to mention nothing a couple of over-the-counter pain relievers hadn't handled once she'd finally taken them. *After* everyone had left the house. She just hadn't been able to bring herself to face all those people. The pitiful stares or judgmental frowns from those who'd no doubt heard about her new attitude toward God. So she'd let Aiden go with Micah and Peggy.

Her friend cocked her head. "It's no wonder with all the stress you've been under. Though, probably not the best move, given your comments about not trusting God to those ladies earlier this week."

"You heard, huh?" Tori worried her bottom lip. She could only imagine how the tongues must've been wagging today.

"Oh, come on, Tori. You'd reached your breaking point and the words tumbled out. I know you didn't really mean them."

Moving her gaze to her son as he continued to bob about in the water, she said, "Actually, I did."

Her friend, who'd spent her life running from God until a few years ago, narrowed her gaze. "You can't be serious. The girl who perpetually begged me to give God a chance?" One dark eyebrow arched. "You're partially responsible for me coming to faith in Jesus. Now you're turning your back on Him?"

Tori stiffened her spine and looked her friend in the eye. "I don't expect you to understand."

"Oh, I don't, huh?" Gloriana leaned forward, resting her arms on the table. "Obviously, you've forgotten who you're talking to. Look, Tori, I know you've had a very rough week. That you've faced more than your fair share of loss in recent years. It stands to reason that you'd be hurting and angry. But be aware, my friend, while you might try to run *from* God, you can't outrun Him. And I know this for a fact because He loved me enough to pursue me even when I chose not to trust Him."

"Uncle Micah!"

Tori jerked at Aiden's declaration.

"Hey, champ." Micah continued across the stone-paved patio toward his nephew. "I hear you've been practicing your handstands." He perched his hands on his hips.

"Uh-huh. Wanna see?"

"I sure do."

"He's so good with Aiden," Gloriana mumbled.

"He is." Tori watched the man who'd done so much for the both of them. Been her rock when she'd fallen to pieces. And stirred feelings she wasn't sure she should have for her brother-in-law. "Sometimes I wonder what we'd do without him."

"He's easy on the eyes, too."

As Micah moved to the side of the pool, Tori jerked her

gaze to her friend's. "Stop that!" she whispered. Not that she didn't agree. "He's my brother-in-law."

"And you're widowed." Her friend lifted a shoulder. "Just sayin'."

"Well, stop it! We are friends and nothing more."

Leaning back in her chair, Gloriana crossed her arms. "How long are you going to keep telling yourself that?"

Her friend knew her too well. First, Gloriana called her out on her lack of faith, and now this. With friends like her, who needed enemies.

It had been a long time since Micah had had so much fun at a birthday party. Seeing Tori enjoying herself for a change did his heart good. Much better than the weariness that seemed to overtake her whenever they sat down to mentally inventory her house. This party had given her something besides recovering from the fire to focus on. And she'd done a great job.

If only he could persuade her to come back to church. She'd missed the last two weeks. Now he couldn't help wondering what excuse she'd come up with tomorrow. And whether or not her son would buy it.

Today, though, under a cloudless sky, fifteen water-logged kiddos sat around a picnic table on the patio in their swimsuits, watching Aiden open his gifts while stuffing themselves silly with chocolate cake. Meanwhile, Micah kept eyeing the driveway, eagerly anticipating Aiden's birthday surprise. Gabriel Vaughn, an old friend of Micah's and the local veterinarian, should be arriving any moment.

Aiden gasped as he tore wrapping paper from the next gift. "Yay! A Spider-Man!" He held up the box containing the action figure. "The fire got my other one."

And that seemed to have been the case with many of the

gifts his friends had given him. Sad as it was, it had probably made shopping a lot easier.

"Tell Maddy and Connor thank you," Tori prompted,
nodding toward Jake and Alli Walker's kiddos.

"Thank you."

"Now it's time for Gigi's present." Clad in a denim shorts
and a bright pink tank top, Tori picked up a colorful gift
bag brimming with yellow and red tissue paper and set
it beside him, smoothing a hand over his still-damp hair.

The kid wasted no time tossing the paper aside. Then
frowned when he pulled the bicycle helmet from the bag.
"But I don't have a bike anymore, Gigi." It, too, had been
taken by the fire.

"Oh, really?" Micah's mother perched a fist on her hip.
"That's not what I heard."

Hank emerged from the house then, bringing with him
a red-and-black bicycle with training wheels.

As his friends began to gasp, Aiden turned just as Hank
neared.

"A bike!" The boy jumped from the table. Inspecting his
gift, he said, "Mama, I got a new bike!"

Tori smiled like the proud mother she was, no doubt
pleased that Aiden was so happy with her gift. "I know."
She moved beside him. "Do you like it?"

Taking hold of the handlebars, he squeezed the coaster
brake. "Uh-huh."

The sound of a vehicle had Micah looking to the driveway. The sight of Gabriel's pickup truck made him smile.
Right on time.

He caught Aiden and Tori's attention. "I'll be right back."

Breaking into a jog, he headed for the house, veering
left to the driveway as Gabriel stepped from the vehicle,
holding a golden-blond ball of fur.

Micah petted the pup, his heart thudding with excitement. "You're even cuter than the first time I saw you." He'd contacted his veterinarian friend last week to see if he'd known of any puppies, and this little golden retriever had fit the bill perfectly.

"She's only wearing a leashed collar right now," said Gabriel, "but I recommend you get her a harness as soon as possible. It'll be harder for her to squirm out of." Passing the seven-week-old pup to Micah, Gabriel rubbed its head. "Isn't that right, cutie pie."

"I already got one." Micah eyed his friend. "It's in my room, along with the crate and other supplies you suggested."

Gabriel smiled. "Sounds like you're ready to go then."

Micah was grinning so big, his cheeks hurt. Aiden was going to be so excited. "Thanks for bringing her by."

"No problem. Y'all have fun." With a wave, Gabriel climbed back into his truck.

Turning, Micah nuzzled the bundle in his arms. "Let's go meet your new best friend."

Noticing that Tori and his mother were watching him as he returned to the backyard, he stopped to set the puppy on the ground and then took hold of her leash as he stood. Aiden was going to be beside himself.

While the little fur ball tugged on the leash, Micah fixed his eyes on the boy as they neared, eager to see Aiden's reaction. And Micah knew just the moment his nephew spotted the dog.

Aiden's dark eyes went wide. "A puppy!"

Suddenly, the leash went slack and Micah heard someone say, "Uh-oh."

He looked down to see the pooch bounding across the patio and into the grass. Meanwhile, its collar remained attached to the leash Micah still held.

Aiden took off after the dog, a few of his friends giving chase with him, which only made the dog run faster.

Regaining his wits, Micah caught up to the kids. "Don't chase her, guys. She'll think it's a game and we'll never catch her."

"You get her, Uncle Micah."

"I'm doing my best, buddy, but I need you and your friends to stand back, please." Finally, he neared the little minx when she paused to sniff around his mother's flower bed. Yet as he went to grab her, the nimble little thing slipped away, happy to continue the game.

While the kids giggled, he saw Tori march into the grass, looking none too happy.

"Everybody freeze." She used her teacher voice, so not one child—or adult—dared to even flinch.

Inching in the direction of the inquisitive animal, she said, "What's its name?"

Micah kept his gaze trained on the dog. "She doesn't have one yet."

Tori slowly lowered herself until she was sitting cross-legged on the grass. "Aren't you a cute little thing?" She patted her legs and the blond bundle of energy bounded toward her. "Come here," Tori coaxed, holding her arms wide. A split second later, the dog leaped into her lap and Tori scooped it into her embrace.

The kids cheered.

"Aiden, you and your friends stay right where you are." Micah started over to Tori, reaching her as she made it to her feet. The dog licked her face.

With a firm hold on the pup, she glared at Micah. "I hope you're going to tell me this dog is yours."

The excitement he'd felt only minutes ago evaporated faster than a water droplet on hot pavement. "Not exactly."

Suddenly his great gift idea didn't seem so great. Perhaps he should have checked with Tori first.

"Then whose is it?"

Oh, boy. He'd better make this good. "It's a gift. For your son. The boy you love more than anything in this world." A little schmoozing never hurt.

Her brow puckered. "Let me get this straight." She lowered her voice to a whisper, her blue eyes boring into him. "You got my son a puppy without asking me first?"

Keeping his own voice low, he said, "Come on, little boys and dogs go hand in hand. She'll be Aiden's constant companion. His best friend."

"One that needs to be fed and watered, not to mention house-broken."

"I plan to help him." He cleared his throat. "That is, assuming you allow me to give her to him. Otherwise, I guess I'll just have to keep her myself." Oh, boy. Now he was digging himself a hole. If Tori wouldn't allow Aiden to have the pup, Micah would be stuck with her. And that would never work if he got the job in College Station.

"Mama, we want to play with the doggie," Aiden said from somewhere behind Micah.

Tori looked from Micah to the dog and back again. "You promise to help Aiden train her?"

"Planned on it all along."

Digging her fingers into the plush fur, she sighed. "I guess you'd better give him your present then." She handed him the pup.

"Thank you, Tori."

"I hope I won't regret this."

Holding the tiny fur ball against his chest, he said, "You won't. I promise. This was my idea and I plan to teach Aiden everything he needs to know about caring for a dog."

He turned to the kids. "Hey, Aiden. Come meet your birthday present."

His nephew's face lit up like a Fourth of July sparkler. "Really?"

"Yes. Now, come here."

The boy raced toward Micah, his friends in tow, which seemed to send Tori into teacher mode again.

"Everyone sit crisscross applesauce in a circle, please," she said.

"Good idea." Micah nuzzled the pup's soft fur. "A human barrier to prevent this one from escaping."

By the time all the kids left an hour later, the puppy had fallen asleep in Aiden's lap and at least half of the parents were annoyed with Micah after their children begged for a puppy.

Now, while his mother and Tori cleaned up the party mess, Micah sat on the floor in the living room, showing Aiden the supplies he'd purchased and explained that having a dog was a big responsibility. Though he wasn't sure how much Aiden really understood.

"The first thing we're going to do is put this harness on her so she can't escape when she's on her leash."

"Yeah, cuz I don't want her to run away," Aiden said as Micah eased it over the dog's head before slipping her paws through the leg holes.

Then, after checking to make sure the harness fit properly, Micah buckled it. "I think you're good to go, bud." Hands perched on his thighs, Micah watched the puppy lick the boy again. "So what are you going to name her?"

Aiden's brow furrowed. "I don't know."

Out of the corner of his eye, Micah saw Tori watching them. "I thought you were cleaning up."

"We're done." She started toward them. "Aiden, how'd you like to head back outside and try out your new bike?"

"Sure." He looked up at her. "Can my puppy come?"

"Yes. But you need to change out of your swimsuit and into some clothes first."

"Okay." He awkwardly palmed the dog's face. "Wanna come see our room?"

"We'll show her around later," Tori said. "You go get changed."

Standing, he looked up at his mother. "Will you watch her while I'm gone?"

"Yes, I will."

While Aiden bounded up the stairs along the far wall, Tori scooped up the pup and settled on the sofa. Rubbing her hands over the dog, she glanced Micah's way. "I'm sorry for giving you a hard time about the dog."

Standing, he shook his head. "No, you're right. I should have asked you first. I guess I was just so fixated on it being a surprise."

"In that case, mission accomplished." Tori continued to pet the dog. "She's so adorable. Where did you get her?"

"I contacted Gabriel a couple of weeks ago, letting him know I was looking for a puppy. Turned out, one of his clients' golden recently had a litter."

Raising the pup so they were eye to eye, Tori said, "You're probably missing your mama and siblings, aren't you?" She nuzzled her nose against the pup's neck. "Between her and the bike, I think our boy is pretty happy."

Micah liked the way she'd said "our boy."

Hoping to take advantage of her good mood, he said, "I know something else that would make him happy."

Cradling the now sleeping puppy in her arms, Tori looked up at him. "What's that?"

"You taking him to church."

Her smile faded, her gaze falling away. "God and I still aren't on speaking terms."

"You sure about that? Or are you just giving Him the silent treatment?"

She glared at him then. "You know, you can be really annoying sometimes, Stallings."

"Right back atcha, Stallings."

Her scowl had him dropping beside her. "Look, I'm not trying to argue with you, Tori. If you want to be mad at God, fine. But I'm not going to enable you. No more feigning a head or stomachache. You need to be honest with your son."

"And what if he wants to stay home with me?"

Micah shrugged. "Your call. You can either lead by example or do the whole 'do as I say, not as I do.'"

"I'm ready!" Aiden bounded down the steps.

"Good deal." Micah stood, his gaze drifting to Tori. "I assume you're going to join us."

Still holding the dog, she pushed to her feet. "Of course. It was my idea."

He quirked a brow. "And the other aspect of our conversation?"

Tori hiked her chin a notch. "I'll take it under consideration. But I'm not making any promises."

As they headed outside, Micah took solace that she hadn't said no. He'd have to wait to see how things played out tomorrow.

Chapter Five

Tori walked into her favorite arts and crafts store in Brenham the second Saturday in October, only to be met with row after row of holiday décor. Christmas had always been her favorite holiday. As a little girl, she would start begging her parents to put up the tree and other decorations before the Thanksgiving turkey had even been put away. Then her pleas would continue for at least two more weeks before her wish was fulfilled.

Needless to say, once she and Joel had married, her tree went up no later than Thanksgiving weekend.

This year would be different, though. Not only was she homeless, all of her decorations and cherished ornaments were gone. Tears stung her eyes. Some irreplaceable, like the one marking Aiden's first Christmas and the one with his tiny handprint they'd made at church.

This week had marked one month since the fire. And despite an inch of rain last week, they still had a long way to go. It frustrated her that she wasn't any closer to rebuilding their lives than she had been the day she'd learned their home was gone. It wasn't like Hope Crossing had a big housing market. At last check, there were only two listings. One was way out of her price range and the second would need so much work that she may as well build new. But building came with its own set of issues.

It was enough to drive a woman to eat an entire box of chocolates. And she'd certainly considered it. Multiple times.

She sucked in a breath, reminding herself she was on a mission. One that was much easier to handle while Aiden was with Micah. The elementary school's annual Holiday Movie Night was less than seven weeks away. Normally, she would've started putting her plans into action a month ago. And while her principal had offered to have someone else take over the event, Tori had argued against the notion, welcoming the chance to have something other than her housing situation to occupy her thoughts.

Besides, the event was a favorite for both kids and their parents. An opportunity to enjoy the holiday season as a family with snacks, crafts, photos and, of course, a movie. This year, at her urging, they were adding a Secret Santa Shop that would give kids an opportunity to do their own Christmas shopping at kid-friendly prices. So, she couldn't, in good conscience, pass the event off to someone else.

Eyeing her list, she pushed her cart toward the craft section, in search of the items they would need to make picture frames. A couple of years ago, the school had constructed their own Polar Express train engine. Each year, they would change the numbers on it to reflect the year and then create a snowy backdrop where the kids and their families would have their pictures taken as a memento of the event.

After gathering what she needed, she continued to roam aisle after aisle, as was her habit. And as instrumental music spilled from overhead speakers, she found herself humming "O Come All Ye Faithful." Until she caught sight of a large Christmas display in the middle of the aisle. Santas, reindeer and snowmen in all shapes and sizes were situated among rustic signs that read Merry Christmas and Joy to the World, poinsettias, colorful ribbon and sparkling greenery filling every space in between.

Save for wringing her hands, she seemed helpless to move, her gaze fixed on the vignette while snapshots of Christmases past played across her mind. Her vision blurred. Her chin began to tremble as heat washed over her. And she couldn't seem to catch her breath. She just stood there staring, tears dripping from her chin and feeling helpless to stop.

"Tori? Are you all right?"

The voice. It was familiar. A hand touched her elbow and she jumped.

"Tori?" The woman stepped in front of her. "It's me. Jillian."

Tori gasped for air. "Jillian?" Through tears, she looked at the woman she'd come to think of as a friend. Then she noticed the infant girl staring up at her from the cart. "I'm sorry. I-I have to go." She retrieved her purse from her buggy, but Jillian grabbed hold of her arm.

"What's wrong, Tori? Please, let me help."

Frantically swiping tears from her cheeks with her other hand, Tori managed to break free. "N-nothing. I just need to go." With that, she abandoned her cart in the aisle, and hurried away in what she hoped was the direction of the exit.

Outside, the hot, humid air made it even more difficult to breathe.

Locating her vehicle, she hit the fob to unlock it, opened the door and threw herself inside. After cranking the A/C, she buckled her seat belt and sped out of the parking lot.

Soon, the countryside stretched to her left and right. And though she knew where she was, she had no idea where she was going. She couldn't go back to Peggy's. Not in this state.

This is all Your *fault*. Her knuckles were white as she gripped the steering wheel.

Instinct must have taken over because the next thing she knew she was driving down the familiar road she'd traversed most of her life. Continuing on to her driveway, she pulled in, parked and got out.

The smoky smell she'd anticipated was no more. Though the surrounding woods—charred and dying—were a testament to the fire's fury.

Her gut burned as she approached the barren piece of land where her home had once sat. A dozer had cleared the ashes, and since they'd had concerns about the integrity of the chimney, it had been dismantled and also removed. Her heart broke as she looked around. One would never know this plot of land had been host to someone's home for more than a century.

She moved to the center of the empty spot, her nostrils flaring as her chest rose and fell. "I hope You're happy," she shouted toward the heavens. "You've taken *everything* from me." Her fists balled at her sides. "Everything except my son, and so help me, if You touch one hair on his head—" Tears poured down her cheeks at the thought. "If You take Aiden, You may as well take me, too, because I can't do this anymore." She all but screamed the words.

A warm breeze skittered over her skin, bringing with it the sound of a vehicle.

Glancing over her shoulder, she spotted Micah's truck. *Just great.*

"I had a feeling you might be here." Hands in the pockets of his cargo shorts, he walked toward her minutes later. "Jillian called. Said she was worried about you."

"Where's Aiden?"

"Brady and Kirsten invited him over to play with the twins."

She narrowed her gaze. "And you let him go without asking me?"

"I called multiple times, but you didn't answer. So when Jillian called—" Hands still in his pockets, he shrugged. "She said you were in pretty bad shape. What's going on? And don't give me some flippant remark. I know you too well, Tori. Something set you off at the store. What was it?"

She wrapped her arms around herself, as though they could hold her together, and stared at the sky, blinking. "Christmas decorations. I don't have any."

"So you buy more."

"Not the cherished ornaments. The ones that marked milestones. The ones Aiden made for me throughout the years, the ones with his tiny handprints." Wiping away a tear, she snorted. "And you wonder why I don't want to go to church."

He dragged a hand through his short hair, shaking his head. "I get that you're angry, Tori. I really do." His dark eyes met hers. "But when are you going to stop blaming God and start rebuilding your life?"

The verbal slap had her taking a step back. "How? What does it even look like to *rebuild*—" she made air quotes "—one's life?"

He continued toward her, stepping into her space. "For starters, stop wallowing in self-pity and start thinking about how you want to proceed. Look at your options and then make some decisions. Yes, it's going to be hard, but you don't have to do it alone. I'm more than willing to help you, whether you need a sounding board, advice or anything else." He heaved a sigh. "Tori, your son is looking to you to lead him into this next phase of your lives. Please, don't let him down."

Oh, she would love nothing more than to rail at Micah. But she couldn't. Because as much as she hated to admit it, he was right.

Tilting her head to the sky, she blinked rapidly. "What if I do? Let Aiden down, that is. What if the choices I make aren't the right ones?"

"Then I will be more than happy to point that out to you."

She looked his way, his smirk annoying her. With a playful shove, she said, "Stop trying to rain on my pity party."

Turning, she rubbed her arms as she surveyed the burned-out area. "This place is never going to look the way it used to."

He shook his head. "Not in our lifetime. But God can give beauty for ashes."

While she wished he'd quit bringing God into everything, she knew Micah was right. For Aiden's sake, she had to stop looking back and start moving forward. Even though she had no idea what that might look like.

"This is a good-size kitchen." Micah ran a hand over the quartz countertop in the model home shortly before noon the following Saturday, hoping and praying the visit would present Tori with some inspiration for her new home. "And the fact that it's open to the living space is nice. Allows you to keep an eye on Aiden."

"I suppose." Clad in jeans, a pale pink T-shirt and sandals, she all but sneered. "Though I'm not a fan of those dark cabinets."

He willed himself to remain positive. "Good news. When you build, you get to pick whatever color you want." Watching her wander through the adjoining dining space, arms crossed over her chest, he was glad Aiden was playing with Jeremy and Trevor at their house. When had Tori become so critical?

The same day she'd decided she couldn't trust God anymore.

The grief, he understood. What he couldn't comprehend was why the girl who seemed to bounce back from whatever life threw at her had decided to give up on God. Had losing her home been the proverbial last straw?

Somehow, he had to find a way to bring her back from this precipice of despair. To make her see that God still loved and cared about her. That just because things didn't go the way she'd planned, doesn't mean He'd turned His back on her.

She started into the living space then made a quick right into the hall where a secondary bathroom and two bedrooms were situated. "One of the bedrooms is a little on the small side," she said when she reappeared. "This living space isn't bad, though."

Finally, a positive remark.

"Too bad it doesn't have a fireplace." And just when he thought they might be getting somewhere.

He moved beside her. "Just because there isn't one in this house, doesn't mean you can't have one in yours."

"No telling how much that would cost," she mumbled as she ambled toward the back of the house and the master bedroom.

Momentarily closing his eyes, Micah sucked in a breath. *Lord, I'm trying here. I really am. But I could use Your help.*

"Micah!"

With a jerk, he strode through the living space to join her in the master suite. "Yes?"

Arms wide, she wore an incredulous look. "This bedroom has no closet. Why would you have a master bedroom without a closet?"

Tamping down his frustration, he moved into the spacious master bath. "Because it's in here." He continued across the tiled floor, past the double vanity and shower to open the door to the walk-in closet.

She followed, her brow puckering. "Why is it in the bathroom?"

"Because that's the trend nowadays."

She looked from the closet to the bathroom to the bedroom and back again. "I guess it kind of makes sense. All the mussing and fussing goes on in here and the bedroom stays nice and pretty."

"Something like that, yes." At this point, he'd take what he could get.

After making a second pass through the house, they exited the front door into a pleasant seventy-five-degree day.

He peered down at her. "Would you like to go back to the office and discuss anything with the salesperson?"

"No." She reached for the sunglasses perched atop her head. "But I'm craving a pumpkin spice latte." Slipping the glasses on her face, she said, "You drive, I'll buy."

Finally, something they could agree on.

"Overall thoughts?" He eyed her as he maneuvered his truck out of the parking lot a couple of minutes later. Unfortunately, those sunglasses hid too much.

"Everything in it was so…new. It lacked character."

"What do you call 'character'?"

"Something that makes it unique. Like the beautiful wood moldings that were in my house. The Austin fieldstone fireplace at your mom's."

"Tori, that home is just a model. You get to design *your* home the way *you* want it."

"What if I go through with this, have a house built, and then I don't like it?" She sighed, staring at the traffic ahead. "Maybe I'm just not ready yet."

"Look, it's not like the house is going to appear out of thin air. You'll have a lot of decisions to make before they even pour the slab. So you're looking at about a year before you move in."

She jerked her head his way. "That long?"

"Yes."

Her sigh was rather dramatic. "At this point, Aiden will be in middle school before I'm ready."

Micah could only pray it wouldn't take her that long. Living in the same house with Tori these past six weeks had been difficult enough. Like having your dream car parked in your garage and not being able to do anything but admire it.

Not that he was planning to stay at Mom's forever. Still, he'd do well to keep his feelings in check. Just the way he'd always done. After all, she was his brother's widow.

"I don't suppose you've talked to God about your situation, have you?"

She eyed him across the cab. "You know I'm not on speaking terms with Him."

"Which may be a big part of the problem."

Before she could respond, his phone rang through the truck's speakers. Though he didn't recognize the number, the area code indicated it was relatively close.

He thumbed the button on the steering wheel. "Hello?"

"I'm looking for Micah Stallings."

"This is Micah."

"My name is Craig Dodson, I'm calling from TEEX Brayton Fire Training Field up here in College Station, regarding the program instructor position you applied for."

"Yes, sir." Micah eased off the gas pedal as he neared the strip center, a slow smile pulling at the corners of his mouth.

"I'm sorry to call on a Saturday—"

"No problem." He turned on his blinker.

"We're in the process of lining up preliminary interviews. Our current instructor will be retiring at the end of December, so we're looking at a January start date."

That would be perfect, allowing him to finish out the semester with his current classes.

"Would you be available November first at three?"

He'd have to get a sub for his afternoon classes. "I should be able to arrange that."

"Great. We will see you Wednesday, then. I'll be sending you an email with more information. It'll include my contact information, should you run into a conflict."

"Yes, sir. Thank you."

"Enjoy your Saturday."

The call ended and Micah couldn't seem to stop smiling as he wound his way through the crowded parking lot and into a parking space.

"Congratulations." Tori smiled across the center console.

"Thanks." He turned off the engine and unbuckled his seat belt. "This is just the beginning of the process, though."

"But they called you. That means your résumé made an impression on them."

"I guess. But whether or not I'm the best man for the job remains to be seen."

"Does that mean you'll be moving to College Station?" Her smile was gone now. Though he refused to read anything into it.

"That's the plan. *If* I get the position."

She undid her seat belt. "I'm sure they'll be so impressed, they move you to the top of their list."

"You always did have more faith in me than I have in myself."

Removing her sunglasses, she met his gaze. "Not only are you good at what you do, Micah, you're passionate about it. That alone will make you a prime candidate." There was something in her tone. Something almost imperceptible that had nothing to do with her housing frustrations.

"Is something wrong?" Like maybe she didn't want him to go. That she was coming to think of him as more than just a friend.

Get real, Stallings!

She shook her head. "It's rather selfish, really." Meeting his eyes again, she continued. "You're so good with Aiden. The kind of positive male influence he needs in his life. He's really going to miss you."

Micah's hopes, the ones he'd told himself to keep in check, deflated. Of course it was about Aiden. Micah was, is, and always would be, relegated to the friend zone where Tori was concerned. Joel was the one who'd stolen her heart. Even in death, he still held it.

"We'll cross that bridge *if* and when we get to it. Besides, College Station is only an hour away."

"You're right." Smiling, she reached for the door. "C'mon, let's go celebrate."

Though their discussion had his appetite for his favorite fall beverage waning, he joined her anyway. Now if only his head would tell his heart to keep Tori at arm's length. But he had a feeling that wasn't going to happen.

Chapter Six

❧

In all the years Tori had been bringing Aiden to the church's annual fall festival, she couldn't recall more perfect weather. Temps topping out in the low eighties while wispy clouds drifted aimlessly across a crystal-blue sky made for a spectacular day. If only she didn't feel so awkward and out of place.

That's what you get for going off on a bunch of church ladies.

Surely, everyone had understood how stressed she'd been that day after the fire. Under normal circumstances, she never would have voiced her change of heart toward God. Even if she had decided He wasn't worthy of her trust anymore, she should have kept her thoughts to herself. But then, she hadn't exactly been in her right mind. Sadly, by the time she'd come to that conclusion, the damage had already been done.

Now, here she stood in the shade of a live oak tree, assisting Jillian at the bounce house—Tori taking tickets while Jillian monitored the kids leaping around inside the colorful inflatable—just waiting for someone to call her out. But when Alli Walker—her friend helping head up this year's event—had called this morning to let Tori know the person who'd committed to help Jillian wasn't going to able to make it, Tori hadn't been able to bring herself to say no. Not when this was Jillian's first time attending the event, while Tori had been to just about every fall festival the church had hosted.

Had it been anyone else, Tori might've been more inclined to say no, but since it was Jillian, the same woman who'd witnessed her meltdown at the craft store, she felt the need to redeem herself.

Tori sucked in a breath, the late-afternoon sun playing peek-a-boo through the leaves as she spotted two little girls from her class rushing across the grass in her direction, their faces painted with colorful butterflies and hearts.

"Ms. Stallings!" Aubrey, a dark-haired girl, beamed, her long ponytail swishing from side to side.

Beside her, Kinsley, a bubbly blonde, wore a smile that mirrored her friend's. "We wanna bounce!"

They certainly had the energy for it. "In that case, may I have your tickets?"

They presented them simultaneously.

"All right, girls, take off your shoes and hop inside."

As the noise level inside the inflatable increased, a smiling Jillian inched closer, causing Aggie, her chocolate-brown poodle service dog, to lift her head, seemingly contemplating whether or not Jillian needed assistance.

"I remember loving bounce houses when I was their age." Jillian shook her head, her long auburn ponytail swaying with the movement. "My parents practically had to drag me out. Now, I'm not sure I could find the energy for even a single minute in there."

Meeting her halfway, Tori smiled. "I know what you mean. I get exhausted just watching them."

"Mama!"

Turning, she saw Aiden running her way, his grin stretching from ear to ear while his uncle trailed behind him in a pair of jeans that looked as though they'd been tailor made just for him.

"I won the cake walk." From the look on Aiden's face, it may as well have been the World Series.

"Oooh… Let me see." Only then did she realize Micah was holding something.

"The kid's got good taste." He dipped his head at the contents of the clear plastic container. "He chose Francie Krenek's pumpkin cake."

Tori stooped so she was eye to eye with her son. "Did you know that is my *favorite* cake?"

He nodded. "Uncle Micah told me."

She glanced up at the man who looked ridiculously handsome—not to mention buff—in that black marines T-shirt that fit him just so. "Probably because it's his favorite, too."

"We were hoping you might hold on to it for us," said Micah. "I thought about putting it in the truck, but I'm afraid the frosting will melt."

She reached for the container. "We definitely don't want that. I'll put it on this chair—" she pointed to the hard-plastic one beside the table "—so it'll be in the shade."

"Don't let anybody steal it." Aiden looked up at her, his expression so serious she had to bite back a smile.

"I will guard it with my life." She then offered a small salute.

"We'll be back later." Micah waved as they walked away.

"He adores Aiden, doesn't he?"

Tori turned to find Jillian watching the duo as they left. "Yes, he does. He's the best uncle a kid could ask for." Though Micah was so much more than just an uncle. He probably spent more time with Aiden than some fathers spent with their own kids. And not once had he ever acted as though her son was an imposition.

A group of parents approached and all five kids exited the bounce house, temporarily leaving her and Jillian alone.

"I hope you're not upset with me for contacting Micah that day I saw you in the craft store." Jillian seemed somewhat hesitant. "You were pretty upset. I wanted to make sure someone knew so they could check on you and, well—" she waved a hand "—you two always seem to be together, so he was the first person that came to mind."

"No, I'm not upset. A little embarrassed perhaps." She shrugged. "For some reason, that display reminded me of all the memories I'd lost in the fire. That all my Christmas decorations were gone."

"It triggered you."

Looking at Jillian, she saw the sincerity in her pretty blue eyes. "*Triggered* is a good word for it."

Aggie pushed her way between them, nudging Tori's hand, seemingly encouraging her to pet the canine's soft curls.

"She senses that you're struggling," noted Jillian. "She's trying to distract you by offering comfort."

Tori stooped to the dog's level, giving her a good rub. "You're a pretty smart pup, aren't you, Aggie?"

"This is probably none of my business..." Jillian began, causing Tori to push to her feet. "But I want you to know that I understand what it is to struggle with your faith. To have your world upended and feel as though God has abandoned you."

Tori thought back to that day almost a year ago when Jillian had stood before the church and given her testimony, revealing to the whole congregation the circumstances behind her pregnancy. Tori admired Jillian's courage and strength of character.

"He could've prevented my attacker from getting to me," Jillian continued. "Just like He could have spared your home from those flames. But then I wouldn't have moved to Hope Crossing. And my baby girl wouldn't have an amazing father in Gabriel." She took hold of Tori's hand. "I'm trusting He's got a wonderful, amazing future in store for you, too, Tori."

Nodding, she said, "I understand what you're saying, Jillian, and I appreciate it. But I'm just not there yet. And I don't know when or if I ever will be. This isn't the first time God has let me down. Simply the proverbial straw that broke this camel's back."

Jillian tilted her head. "You and your son are both still here, safe and sound. That's what's most important."

"I know."

"I'm praying for you." Jillian's gaze bore into her. "That God will give you direction moving forward, and that you'll have a change of heart where He's concerned."

"Thank you." Realizing how lame that sounded, she quickly added, "And I mean that sincerely."

"I know you do." Jillian's gaze drifted somewhere behind Tori then her brow puckering in what appeared to be concern. "Aiden and Micah are coming back. And they look like they're in a hurry."

Turning, Tori recognized the intensity in Micah's expression. The determination in his strides as a cool breeze carved its way between them, raising the hair on her arms.

"My pager went off." He halted several feet away while Aiden continued her way. "I need to get to the station."

Tori wound her arms around her middle. Images of that dreadful day when he'd accompanied her to her house to retrieve only her most precious possessions swirled through her head, followed by memories of the military chaplain standing on her porch the day she'd learned Joel was dead.

Somehow managing to swallow around the sudden lump in her throat, she scanned the horizon, searching for smoke. "Wh-where is it?"

"I don't know yet. I just need to go." With a final wave, he turned and jogged away.

Her heart squeezed.

"Mama, I'm hungry," she heard Aiden say beside her. "I want a hot dog."

"Okay, baby." Lowering her arms, she smoothed a hand over his dark hair, her heart racing as she caught a final glimpse of Micah before he threw himself into his pickup. She wanted to rush after him and beg him not to go. Because an unexpected question suddenly played through her mind.

What if he didn't come back?

Micah pulled into the driveway a few minutes before eight that night, eager to hear what all Aiden had done after Micah had to leave the festival. He felt terrible abandoning the kid. The way Aiden had pooched out his bottom lip tugged at Micah's heartstrings. Though that wasn't the image that had been stuck in his head these past few hours. Instead, it had been the look on Tori's face when he'd told her he was leaving. The way she'd hugged herself, as though trying to hold herself together. But why?

The sun had set more than an hour ago, so lights glowed inside the house as he exited his truck and approached the back door. And the way his stomach growled, one would think he hadn't eaten in a week. He sure hoped they'd saved him a piece of that pumpkin cake. Though he might need to shower first. In his rush to get back home before Aiden's bedtime, he'd only rinsed off at the station, leaving him rather odiferous.

He slipped through the kitchen door, half expecting Aiden to greet him. But the only sound he heard was the television's low volume coming from the living room. The kid must be curled up alongside his mama, engrossed in one of his shows.

Continuing through the kitchen, he could see Tori sitting on the sofa. Alone, save for Aiden's pup, Lizzie, curled up beside her.

"How's it going?"

Tori turned his way as he approached, the corners of her mouth lifting somewhat nervously. "You're home." Standing, she muted the television while Lizzie jumped down and hurried toward Micah, tail wagging.

Stooping, he gave the canine a quick scratch.

"I wasn't sure when you'd be back." After setting the remote aside, she crisscrossed her arms, moving her hands up and down as though she was chilled. "How'd it go?"

"It was nothing too bad. Someone's burn pile got out of control."

Tori stiffened, her brow puckering "Burn pile? What were they thinking?"

Rubbing the back of his neck, he said, "Since we've had some rain, they thought the burn ban had been rescinded."

"An inch of rain is nowhere near a drought buster." Her tone held an air of indignation. "Especially after the summer we had."

"I know." Hoping to diffuse her ire, he said, "Where's Aiden?"

"Asleep." The rigid set of her shoulders relaxed a notch, though she continued to hug herself. Something Micah found rather odd. Maybe she was cold. "He had a bath then crashed on the couch about an hour ago, so I put him to bed."

"Guess he wore himself out at the festival."

Her head bobbed. "He sure did. Jeremy and Trevor arrived shortly after you left, so the three of them bounced themselves silly until my shift was over, then they played games and ran all over the place until the event shut down."

Realizing they were alone, he said, "Where's Mom?"

"I'll give you one guess."

"At Hank's?"

Tori confirmed his suspicion with a nod. "Probably helping him with whatever updates he's doing over at his place."

"Again?" Micah dragged a hand through his grimy hair. "The guy must be overhauling his entire house."

With a shrug, she said, "Perhaps he's fixing things up so they're more to your mama's liking."

"Why would he do that?" Micah paused. Come to think of it, Mom and Hank had been growing a lot closer in recent months. Still… "I can't imagine her ever moving out of this house. Can you?"

"She hasn't mentioned anything to me, but you never know."

Glancing at the TV, he saw a fella taking a sledgehammer to someone's kitchen cabinets. "What are you watching?"

"Some home design show. Thought it might help me get my head into the house-building game." One shoulder lifted. "You know, give me some ideas. Maybe spark some interest. I mean Aiden and I can't stay here forever." Her gaze drifted to the fireplace, then traced its stone front all the way up to the twenty-foot cathedral ceiling, looking nothing at all like the confident woman he knew her to be. "Though

I have to say, this place does kind of feel like home. But then, I guess I've spent a good part of my life here."

Yes, she had. Starting with their awkward junior high years when she'd come over to help him with his menagerie of animals. Joel had never paid Tori any mind back then. But then, Micah had heard folks liken her to the ugly duckling that grew into a beautiful swan. Yet while Joel's head had been turned by the swan, Micah had always thought Tori beautiful.

"Not to mention, it doesn't have that cookie-cutter feel like those model homes," she added.

"That's because this is a custom home. My dad designed it." That was all the more reason for his mother to stay.

"Yeah, custom anything is probably out of my price range." Tori's laugh was a nervous one. "Are you hungry?" She rounded the coffee table to brush past him.

"Starving."

Seemingly refusing to look at him, she said, "Why don't you go get cleaned up while I fix you a plate of the chicken enchilada casserole I pulled out of the freezer."

"Sounds good." Hands perched on his hips, he watched her. Something was off here. Tori seemed…uptight. Nervous, even. "Are you okay?" This wasn't like her. Especially not around him.

"Of course." Her sudden smile and over-the-top cheerfulness only ratcheted his concern. Perhaps he could get her to open up over supper.

He turned to leave then paused. "Don't suppose there's any of Aiden's cake left, is there?"

"Yes. I knew you'd be looking forward to it, so I made sure to save you some."

The fact that she'd been thinking of him had his heart thudding. "In that case, I'll meet you in the kitchen in a few."

He hurried to his room, wondering what it would be like to come home to Tori every night. To know that she was waiting for him at home. Not as houseguest but as something much more.

Then he promptly chastised himself. It was Joel she loved, not him. Micah had nothing special to offer a woman like Tori. He was just a simple guy. Boring, his ex-fiancée, Samantha, had said when she'd broken off their engagement. He couldn't hold a candle to the outgoing bull rider who'd swept her off of her feet any more than he could his brother.

Ten minutes later, he headed to the kitchen with a little less bounce in his step than he'd had when he'd left. Though the spicy aroma filling the air had him realizing just how hungry he was.

Tori glanced his way as he entered the room. "That was quick."

"That's because I knew there was food waiting." He inhaled as she pulled a plate holding a large helping of the steaming casserole from the microwave. "Smells delicious."

"Grab a seat then."

"You don't have to tell me twice." He pulled out a chair at the table as she set the plate in front of him. Moments later, he stabbed his first bite, his taste buds doing a happy dance when the spices mingled on his tongue.

Lizzie parked beside him, tail wagging as she watched him while Tori busied herself in the kitchen, seemingly lost in her thoughts, her shoulders slumped. And he couldn't shake the feeling that something was off. But what?

Then it hit him. The festival. Tori's greatest fear when Alli had asked her to help out today was that someone would confront her. Tell her she didn't belong there because of what she'd said to those women after the fire. Had something happened after he'd left?

"Tori?"

She looked up from covering the casserole pan with foil, a pained expression on her face.

"Is something wrong?"

Her smile was a tremulous one.

Shaking her head, she said, "I'm fine."

Abandoning his food, he pushed his chair out and stood to move beside her. "You always were a bad liar. Did something happen at the festival after I left? Did someone say something to you?"

"No." The confidence in that single word said she was telling the truth. Regarding the festival anyway.

He studied her for long moment. "Then what's got you on edge?"

"Nothing." There was that forced cheerfulness again.

"Tori, I have known you far too long for you to be trying to pull the wool over my eyes. Something is wrong and I'd appreciate it if you would just tell me what it is instead of making me guess. Because I'm not going to let you alone until you do."

She glared up at him. "Your persistence is one of the things I've always admired about you. At the moment, though, it's kind of annoying."

"You're obviously trying to hide something from me."

Turning away, she said, "It's ridiculous really." She tossed the towel that was over her shoulder onto the counter.

"Okay. So what is it?"

"Would you, please, go eat your food before Lizzie gets it?"

"If you'll come sit with me and explain what is so ridiculous that it's carving deep worry lines into your forehead."

Her right hand flew to her forehead. Regardless of what was bothering her, vanity still reared its ugly head. And that had him wrestling to keep his chuckle under wraps.

With a huff, she said, "Okay, fine. But if you laugh, so help me, Micah, you will be wearing the rest of the pumpkin cake."

"Wow. Talk about wasting a perfectly good pumpkin cake."

"You are such a brat." She whisked past him and started toward the table. Pausing, she darted a glare over her shoulder. "Are you going to join me or not?"

He returned to his seat, took hold of his fork and dipped it into the cheese-covered deliciousness. "I'm ready when you are."

While he took a big bite, she sucked in a breath, looking everywhere but at him. "I was worried about you."

His chewing slowed and he simply stared at her as his thoughts skidded to a stop. Finally, he swallowed. "Why were you worried about me?"

Once again, she hugged herself. "Firefighting is a dangerous job."

"It can be, yes. But that's never bothered you before. At least, not that I'm aware of. So why today?"

She gripped the sides of her chair, her stare fixed somewhere outside the window. "I guess I never gave it much thought before. But ever since the fire at my place." Lifting a shoulder, she lowered her gaze. "See, I told you it was ridiculous. I just don't think I could bear to lose someone else I cared about."

Micah found himself at a loss for words as emotions tripped over each other, vying for center stage. The fact that she cared that deeply for him. But then, they'd been friends for decades. She loved him, even if it was only as a friend.

Though looking at her pained expression, a part of him wondered if her feelings might run deeper. The way his did.

He reached for her hand. "Tori, you're not being ridiculous. Fear of the unknown is a powerful thing. And from a layman's perspective, I suppose fighting fires does seem scary. That's why we're continually training." Touching a finger to her chin, he encouraged her to look at him.

When she did, he saw the genuine fear in her eyes. Something he'd only seen one other time. That day he'd come home with news that her house was gone. The day she'd turned her back on God, believing He was cause of all her problems. When, in fact, she should be clinging to Him, her anchor during life's storms.

Instead, she'd let go, allowing the waves of life to buffet her.

Somehow, Micah had to help her find her way back to the One who was in control. Even if it meant risking his heart.

Chapter Seven

Tori stabbed a fork into her salad in the teacher's lounge the following Thursday, feeling more than a little sorry for herself. She was in a funk and she didn't know why.

No, that wasn't true. She knew. She just didn't want to acknowledge it.

Micah had come home from his interview yesterday, bubbling over with excitement. Matter of fact, it had been a long time since she'd seen him so animated. Firefighting wasn't just a job for Micah. It was a calling. One she'd been pouting about five days ago. Working herself into a tizzy over a bunch of what-ifs.

Now she felt foolish. Micah was a professional. He'd been right when he'd pointed out that it had never bothered her before. For some reason, she'd gotten inside her head that day, imagining every worst-case scenario. Was it really because of the fire that destroyed her house? Had it heightened her awareness of the danger Micah and firefighters like him faced?

You used to turn your concerns into prayers.

Until God had ignored her pleas and set her and Aiden on an unfamiliar path.

Ugh! She jabbed a bite of chicken. Now she was becoming bitter. For her son's sake, she couldn't allow that to happen.

Her phone vibrated then and she saw Charlene Lockhart's name on the screen. Tori scrambled to answer it. Not only was Charlene an old classmate, she was now Tori's Realtor.

"Charlene. What's up?" She hoped the woman had some good news.

"You answered. I thought I might have to text you."

"I'm on my lunch. What's up?"

"There's a new listing as of last night that I think you might be interested in. Three bedroom, two bath in Hope Crossing proper. It's an older home, but it's been updated. Honestly, I think you'll like it."

Living in town would certainly cut the drive time to both school and Peggy's, meaning Aiden could see his grandmother more often.

She stood to retrieve a pen and paper from the nearby counter. "What's the address?"

Charlene rattled it off as Tori scribbled.

"I think I know that house. One-and-a-half-story Folk Victorian?" Though the millwork wasn't as ornate as what had been on her house. Still…

"Yes. Which is why I think you'll like it."

Excitement bubbled inside Tori, though she knew better than to get her hopes up. "How soon can I see it?"

"When are you available?"

"As soon as school's out. I can have my mother-in-law pick up Aiden."

"I'll let them know right now."

"Great! Thank you, Charlene."

After polishing off her lunch in short order, Tori called Peggy to make arrangements before heading back to her classroom. Then she texted Micah to let him know. For the first time since the fire, she was actually hopeful. A lot of people shied away from older homes, fearing age-related problems, but Tori appreciated their character.

Her phone lit up as her students settled into their seats. A message from Micah.

Sounds promising. I'm praying God will lead you to the home He has for you.

She smiled, knowing that when Micah said he was praying, he truly was. It wasn't just lip service. Perhaps God would listen to him.

Sadly, her afternoon seemed to drag on. But as soon as the last student had been picked up, as well as Aiden, she hurried to her vehicle and drove three blocks to the quaint pale gray house with white trim.

Easing her SUV to a stop behind Charlene's vehicle, Tori took a deep breath and looked around. The nearby homes seemed to indicate the growth of the tiny town with a 1920s Craftsman across the street to a 1970s rambler farther down the road. At least the homes weren't on top of each other.

She opened her door and stepped into the warm afternoon air. Moments later, she slipped through the gate of the scalloped white-picket fence flanked with pink crepe myrtles, her anticipation building.

Charlene appeared at the front door. "Hi, there."

"Hey, Charlene."

"How's your day going?"

"Better after hearing from you."

The pretty blonde Tori had gone to school with waited atop the wooden porch. "I can't wait for you to see the inside. I think you're going to like it."

Tori's excitement amplified as she climbed the two steps. "Then, by all means, lead on."

Charlene spent the next twenty minutes pointing out the home's highlights before allowing Tori to wander on her own.

"Is the yard big enough for an active little boy?" she asked Charlene a while later.

"Let's go see."

They moved out onto the back porch and down the steps to meander the enclosed area.

"This is definitely a lot smaller than we're used to." Tori eyed the pasture beyond the same picket fence that enveloped the entire lot. "But having that pasture there makes it feel larger." She glanced at the Realtor. "Do you suppose there's enough room for a jungle gym?"

Charlene studied the space. "I think so. That is, unless you're talking something really big."

Tori shielded her eyes from the sun as she took in the quaint setting. "I can see myself living here."

"Does that mean you want to make an offer?"

Facing her friend, she said, "Yes. Though I'll need to go home and crunch some numbers. Can I call you in a few hours?"

Charlene nodded. "You have my number."

Excitement propelled Tori all the way back to Peggy's. And no sooner had she pulled into the driveway than Micah arrived.

She exited her vehicle and waited for him to do the same, feeling as though she might burst.

"Well, somebody's looking mighty happy." He smiled as he rounded his truck, backpack slung over one shoulder. "Does this mean you liked the house?"

"I loved it!" She all but squealed like a teenager, which made him chuckle. "I'll be ready to make an offer just as soon as I can come up with one. I need to look over all the insurance paperwork before I toss out a figure."

His smile seemed to mirror her own. "Need any help? Or should I entertain Aiden so you won't be interrupted."

She peered up at him. "Would you mind? Watching him, that is."

"Of course not. Maybe we can wear Lizzie out in the process."

"Excellent plan, Stallings." She started toward the house then stopped. "Please, don't say anything to Aiden about this. I don't want to get his hopes up and then have it fall through."

"I understand. My lips are sealed. But let's think positive, all right?"

"I'm trying." She turned, motioning for him to follow. "Come on."

The aroma of fresh-baked cookies filled the kitchen. Aiden stood on a stool at the counter, clad in one of his grandmother's aprons as he ran a rubber scraper through the bowl in front of him.

"Mama, I helped Gigi make cookies."

"I can tell. They smell delicious. What kind did you make?"

"Chocolate chip." He licked the scraper with bits of dough still clinging to it as his uncle sidled up beside him.

"How about a taste for your favorite uncle?"

"Uh-uh." Aiden shook his head, grinning as though he enjoyed torturing his uncle.

"What's that?" Micah pointed. Then, when Aiden looked away, Micah ran a finger along the inside of the bowl.

Aiden looked at his uncle as he shoved his finger in his mouth. "Hey!"

Licking his lips, Micah said, "What do you say we take Lizzie outside and you can ride your bike?"

"Yeah!"

While Aiden worked to remove the apron, Peggy looked Tori's way. "Well…how'd it go?"

"I think it's the one." She couldn't seem to stop smiling. "I need to work up an offer, though. So, I need to hurry and get on my laptop and figure some things out."

"Then, by all means." Peggy shooed her with her hands. "Micah and I can handle Aiden."

Tori hurried upstairs and crawled onto her bed with her laptop. While it might be a stretch, she was hoping to offer the owners asking price. But first she needed to be certain she could pull it off. And thirty minutes later, she felt confident.

She was about to call Charlene when her phone rang. Seeing the woman's name on the screen, she answered with, "I was just about to call you."

"Tori, I'm afraid I have some bad news."

Her heart skidded to a stop. No. This house was meant for her. She knew it in her bones. Please, no.

"The sellers received an offer while we were at the house. And I'm sorry to say, they accepted it."

"But why would they do that? They could have gotten a better offer. Even had a bidding war." Not that that would have been to her advantage.

"I'm as disappointed as you are, Tori. Really, I am."

Somehow she doubted that. Charlene had a home. One she shared with her adoring husband she'd reunited with and their daughter.

With a sigh, Tori said, "Thanks for letting me know."

"If I hear of anything else, I will contact you right away."

As if houses went on the market every day in Hope Crossing. "Thank you."

Ending the call, Tori flopped back on the bed, tears

stinging her eyes as the desire to scream into her pillow almost overwhelmed her. Why would God do that? Get her hopes up only to have them squashed?

I'm praying God will lead you to the home He has for you.

Evidently God hadn't heard Micah's prayer either.

A knock sounded at her door.

She sat up, swiping her eyes in case it was Aiden. She didn't want him to see her cry.

"Who is it?"

"Micah. I'm checking to see if you need any help."

Easing off of the bed, she moved to the door and opened it.

The moment he looked at her, his smile evaporated. "What's wrong?"

Her chin began to tremble. "Someone else made an offer." Tears filled her eyes. "And they accepted it."

As her tears fell in earnest, he stepped closer and enveloped her in his strong arms. "I'm so sorry."

She wound her arms around his waist and held on tight, absorbing the strength he so freely offered, until her tears ceased.

When she finally released her hold, she looked up at him. "Evidently God doesn't listen to you either."

His brow puckered. "What do you mean?"

"You said you'd be praying."

"And I did. That God would lead you to the home *He* has for you. I guess this wasn't the one."

"But it was perfect. I could envision myself and Aiden living there."

"Maybe so. But God sees the big picture, Tori."

"What is that supposed to mean?"

"He has a home for the two of you. And it'll be better

than anything you've imagined. But it'll happen in His timing."

"I know you believe that. And there was a time I might have, too. But you're going to have to have enough faith for both of us, because I just don't have the energy anymore."

He held her chin between his thumb and forefinger and encouraged her to look at him. And the intensity of his gaze was unlike anything she'd seen before.

"If that's what it takes, Tori, then that's precisely what I'll do."

With two tumultuous months barely in her rearview mirror, the last thing Tori needed was to be reminded of another difficult time. Yet the Hope Crossing community had been set on honoring one of their fallen heroes with a Veterans Day ceremony at the Joel Stallings Memorial Park and, of course, they wanted the family in attendance.

Despite everything she'd been through of late, Tori had held her head high and remained strong, no matter how many people hugged her and, once again, offered their condolences. Micah knew they meant well, but who wanted to be reminded of the death of a spouse year after year in the public square? Especially now, when she was still dealing with the loss of her home. Not to mention losing out on that house in town last week.

Micah shook his head. He'd bent God's ear a good bit on that one. Because, while he trusted God's plan, seeing Tori get her hopes up only to have them dashed had been difficult to watch. So he'd been trying to think of some way to lift her spirits ever since. Something that would encourage her and, hopefully, make her smile instead of playing Whac-A-Mole with her wellbeing. And now that the ceremony was over, he was ready to do just that.

Hands in the pockets of his softshell jacket while oak trees towered overhead, he shifted his gaze from Aiden—who was dangling from a nearby climbing apparatus while his friends Jeremy and Trevor clamored to do the same—to the pale gray clouds obscuring the sun. Instead of bringing any rain, though, they only added to today's somber mood. At least God had blessed them with a small amount of rain in October and then again earlier this week. No drought-busters, by any means, but more than they'd had since spring.

"How long do you think it'll take us to pry them away from that thing?" Brady, an army veteran, sidled up beside him, eyeing the three boys.

"The fact that they're going home together should help." Micah eyed his friend. "Thanks again for offering to keep Aiden." The original plan had been for his grandmother to take him home with her. But since Mom and Hank needed to make a run to the home improvement center in Brenham, Kirsten and Brady had said Aiden could go home with them.

"Hey, when you already have two, one more is no big deal."

"Yeah, but with Kirsten pregnant, I hate to put too much on her."

"Ah, she's past all that morning sickness now. Besides, the boys get along great." Hands in the pockets of his jeans, Brady rocked back on the heels of his boots. "Does Tori know about your plans?"

"Not yet." Micah shook his head. "And hopefully she won't balk when I spring them on her."

With a nod, Brady said, "I guess we'll know pretty quick. She and Kirsten are headed this way."

Micah was pleased when he saw Tori smiling as she

spoke with Brady's wife. Wearing a dark green shirt, skinny jeans and boots, topped off with a gray cardigan, her blond hair bouncing around her shoulders, she all but took his breath away.

Still, there was a sadness about her. One most people wouldn't notice. Her smile didn't quite reach her eyes. Eyes that no longer sparkled.

He hoped today might change that.

"I don't know about y'all, but I'm ready to blow this Popsicle stand." Hands fisted in the pockets of her sweater, she looked from Micah and Brady to the trio of active boys. "I have to make a run to the craft store today."

Something she'd been dragging her feet over since the meltdown she'd had during her last visit, which was why Micah had added it to his list.

Tori stepped closer to the playground. "Aiden, come on. It's time to go."

"Aww." The boy whined. "I'm having fun."

"Sorry, we have things to do today."

"Why don't you let him come home with us?" Kirsten offered as though it was her idea. "With Aiden there to entertain the boys, perhaps I can work on clearing out what will eventually be the nursery."

Tori appeared somewhat hesitant. "I—"

"What's going on?" Hank approached, Mom at his side, and Micah couldn't help noticing they were holding hands. A move that had Micah taking a mental step back. Until he saw the smile on his mother's face. Widowed when she was only in her late fifties, she still had plenty of life ahead of her. And as far as men went, Hank was a good one.

"We're about to head home," said Brady.

"I think we're off, too." Micah looked at Tori. He'd made sure he was the one to drive her and Aiden to this morning's event so there'd be no questions when it came time to leave. Of course, she'd probably protest when she realized he wasn't taking her home.

Tori glanced at her son. "Aiden, how would you like to go home with Jeremy and Trevor for a while?"

The kid's eyes went wide, right along with his friends'. "Can I?" He looked from his mother to Micah then Brady and Kirsten.

"Sure," said Brady. "Let's go."

Micah looked at Tori. "You ready?"

"Yep."

As they pulled out of the parking lot a short time later, he said, "So. What did you think?"

"That it was like every other Veterans Day ceremony they've had. I mean I appreciate they want to remember Joel, but that's why they named the park after him. They don't need to keep rehashing things."

"Yeah, it was rather anticlimactic." He paused at the stoplight then continued straight instead of turning.

"Where are you going?"

He could feel her staring at him. "You said you needed to go to the craft store."

"Yes, but I was—I mean you don't have to..." With a sigh, she leaned back in her seat. "How did you know I was dreading going back there?"

"Because I know you. You've been procrastinating."

Staring out the window, she said, "I was afraid I might have another meltdown."

"Well, now you've got me to distract you, embarrass you. Whatever it takes."

After a long pause, she said, "Micah, what would I do without you?"

"Hopefully you'll never have to find out." Though the

remark came across as flippant, there was more truth in there than Tori probably realized.

"Mind if I turn on some music?"

"Go right ahead."

She punched the button and, seconds later, Zach Williams's rendition of "Run, Run, Rudolph" blared through the speakers.

"Seriously?" She glared at him. "Christmas music already?"

"Says the woman who starts watching Christmas movies in October." Though, not so much this year.

As the song continued to play, she began shimmying in her seat, snapping her fingers and singing along. So, by the time they reached the store, Tori was in a much better mood. They quickly grabbed the items on her list, though with festive holiday decorations scattered throughout the store, the lure to browse seemed too much for her to resist.

As they passed an aisle with stockings, Micah touched her elbow, encouraging her to stop. "Want to pick out a stocking for Aiden?"

Following his gaze, she said, "You're right. I forgot he'll need a new one."

"Let's go have a look then. Because once Thanksgiving hits, these will be picked over."

Soon, she was oohing and aahing her way down the aisle. "Oh, Micah, look." Plucking a stocking from the display, she held it up. "This one has a fire truck."

He couldn't help smiling. Not exactly what he would've picked for Aiden.

"This is perfect for you," she continued.

"Me?"

"Yes, you." She placed it in the cart. "I just need to find someone to embroider your name on it."

"We're supposed to be getting a stocking for Aiden."

"One is never too old for a stocking. Like they say, the best things come in small packages."

Kind of like her.

The thought blazed through his mind before he could stop it. And that didn't bode well for the rest of the day.

After locating just the right stocking for Aiden—one with a puppy on it—they continued to stroll the aisles while Christmas carols played overhead. And by the time they made it to the checkout, their cart was full.

As they made their way back to his truck a short time later, he said, "Looks like somebody rediscovered their Christmas spirit."

Smiling, she moved one bag after another into the back seat. "Thanks to you." She looked up at him as the sun finally appeared. "You give me the courage to face my fears."

He stared into her beautiful eyes, longing to kiss her. Instead, he said, "Hungry?"

"Getting there. Why?"

"Hop in the truck and find out."

Her smile was a playful one. "Got any more Christmas music?"

He wiggled his phone. "Right here."

"Let's go, then."

He couldn't help smiling at her enthusiasm because he had even more in store for her. Lunch at her favorite Mexican grill, a trip to her favorite fragrance store for candles and those lotions she liked. Whatever it took to see Tori smile.

As they hopped onto the highway, tires humming against the pavement as For King and Country's "The Little Drummer Boy" blasted from the speakers, he was reminded of the last time he'd gone to such lengths to please a woman.

The night he'd proposed to Samantha, he'd pulled out all the stops. Roses. The finest restaurant in town. The ring. Her surprise had quickly morphed into elation. She couldn't wait to start planning their wedding. Looking back, he realized that everything they'd done from that night forward had revolved around that one event. Yet they'd never talked about their future.

Perhaps that was why she'd dumped him for that bull rider less than two months later. The charismatic fella had reminded Micah of Joel. The kind of guy who liked being the center of attention. And Samantha had been more than happy to give him hers. Micah hadn't been able to compete with him any more than he could with Joel.

He'd do well to remember that. Especially when his feelings for Tori seemed to be growing stronger with each passing day. If he didn't watch himself, he'd end up in a world of hurt once again. Making that position in College Station even more desirable.

Chapter Eight

Tori couldn't remember the last time someone had gone to such lengths to do something special for her. That a man had made her feel as though she mattered. Yet that was exactly what Micah had done. And so much more. He'd rekindled her love for Christmas. By the time they'd returned home late last Saturday from his surprise shopping trip, she'd not only bought Christmas stockings but numerous decorations, candles—in her favorite holiday scent—and even a few gifts. Now, she could hardly wait for the holidays.

First things first, though. Thanksgiving was less than a week away. Then she'd be headlong into final preparations for the Holiday Movie Night at school.

But this night was all about her friend Gloriana. Her brother and sister-in-law, Hawkins and Annalise, were hosting a gender reveal party, and Tori and Micah had been invited.

While she was happy for her friend, Tori was also a tad envious. As an only child, she'd always longed to have multiple children. Something Joel had said he'd wanted, too. But when a couple spends more time apart than together... Now, as a thirty-six-year-old widow, the likelihood of that dream coming true was slim to none.

At least she had Aiden. And now that she'd rediscovered her holiday spirit, she was determined to make this one of the best Christmases ever for him. Sure, it would be nice to have their own home to celebrate in, but unless something were to drop in her lap, she was going to put her worries over that on a back burner until the new year.

Now, in her upstairs bedroom at Peggy's late Saturday afternoon, she threaded a gold stud earring through each earlobe then stood in front of the full-length mirror for a final inspection. While her wardrobe had grown somewhat, she still struggled to come up with outfits for special occasions like this. But since the event was being held in the barn at the Christmas tree farm, she'd managed to pull together a simple outfit consisting of a white button-down shirt topped with a teal pullover sweater over skinny jeans and a pair of brown suede booties.

Deciding it would do, she grabbed the barn coat she'd purchased last weekend, in case she needed it later tonight. She then hurried downstairs as darkness descended, where she found Aiden staring out of one of the large windows in the living room, Lizzie at his side.

"Are you watching for your friends?" She rubbed the pup's head while Aiden continued to gape. Since Brady and Kirsten were also attending the party, Peggy had suggested Hank bring the twins over.

"Uh-huh."

Smoothing a hand over his hair, she said, "They'll be here shortly."

After dropping a kiss atop his head and inhaling that little boy scent, she continued into the kitchen to find Micah waiting for her.

"I'm sorry it took me so long." She set her purse and jacket atop the counter. "I have the hardest time figuring out what to wear these days." Only then did she notice the lopsided grin on his face as he stared at her. "What?"

"First of all, you're not late. And even if you were—" his seemingly appreciative gaze flitted over her "—I'd say it was worth the wait."

Heat suffused her cheeks as her heart began to race. She wasn't used to getting compliments on her appearance. Particularly from a man. An incredibly attractive one at that. One she seemed to have a growing awareness of.

"Thank you."

"Jeremy and Trevor are here!" Aiden's proclamation jolted her back to her senses.

Micah chuckled. "We'll head out once the boys are settled."

Ten minutes later, they were on the road. Naturally, Aiden was so thrilled to have his friends over that he'd barely acknowledged their departure. Her baby was growing up so fast. She wished he'd stay little. At least for a while longer.

"You're mighty quiet over there." Only minutes into their journey, Micah eyed her from the driver's seat of his pickup. "What are you moping about?"

How did he know she was feeling sorry for herself?

Because Micah knows you like the back of his hand.

"Just the fact that, every time I turn around, Aiden seems to need me less and less."

Snorting, he shook his head. "Tori, like it or not, the kid's growing up. Now that he's in school, it's natural he'd want to spread his wings."

"His friends hold more appeal than I do."

"You'd better buckle your seat belt then, because the older he gets, the more time he'll want to spend with his friends and away from you. Just like you and I did." Eyes fixed on the headlight-illuminated road in front of them, he added, "But trust me, a boy never outgrows needing his mama."

She felt the corners of her mouth twitch. "Thank you for saying that."

"I'm not just *saying* anything. I'm speaking from experience." Amid a glow from the truck's console, he shot her a wink that made her insides flutter.

What was wrong with her? One would think she and Micah were on a date with the way she was behaving. All these nonsensical thoughts and reactions.

Thankfully, they were almost to Hawkins and Annalise's. And when they pulled into the drive, Tori couldn't help smiling. The place was already decked out for the Christmas tree farm's opening the day after Thanksgiving. Greenery and tiny white lights adorned the porch of the couple's quaint farmhouse to their left while, to their right, icicle lights dangled from the barn's eaves.

Micah parked alongside three other vehicles.

"If this place doesn't get one into the Christmas spirit, nothing will," Tori said as she exited the pickup.

"That's for sure." Micah rounded the front of the vehicle to meet her.

The barn's porch served as the check-in point for tree farm guests with a walk-up window and a small store beyond the double doors. Reclaimed wood from the original barn destroyed by a storm only weeks before the tree farm's grand opening two years ago now adorned the porch's back wall, while rocking chairs, garland-wrapped wood posts and an illuminated vintage snowman created an inviting space for guests. And everywhere she looked, there were lights, reminding Tori of the way Micah's house used to look during the holiday season.

She nudged him with her elbow. "I remember the light displays your folks used to do."

Nodding, he said, "People from all around would drive out to our place just for a glimpse of them." He looked at her now. "Dad was pretty low-key most of the time, but he loved doing those lights. As soon as they went up one year, he'd start planning for the next."

"He brought joy to a lot of people. Too bad Aiden never got to see them. He loves Christmas lights."

"Yeah, well, he comes by it honestly."

Gravel crunched beneath their feet.

"You used to help your dad put them up, didn't you?"

"Every year."

Settling a hand atop his arm, she stopped. "I don't suppose you still have the lights, do you?"

"Sure. That is, unless Mom got rid of them. Otherwise, they're out in the barn."

Unable to contain her smile, she said, "What would you think about you and me recreating one of your father's displays? Aiden would love it."

Micah stared at her. "It's a lot of work."

She shrugged. "We're both off school this week, so we've got the time. It would also help keep Aiden entertained."

Micah seemed to ponder her suggestion for a moment before the corners of his mouth lifted. "You know, that actually sounds kind of fun. Assuming we still have the lights."

"If not, I'd be willing to buy more."

"Yeah." He nodded. "Me, too."

Headlights had them eyeing the entrance as two more vehicles pulled into the drive.

"That's Gabriel and Jillian." Shielding his eyes, Micah pointed to the maroon pickup in the lead. "Jake and Alli are bringing up the rear."

"Well, they do have three kids now, so breaking away is probably a little more challenging."

After greeting their friends, they continued on to the barn as a group, the cool air settling around them as they moved beyond the porch and past the vintage-red Christmas tree truck parked several feet away. Then they meandered toward the large room at the back of the barn that was used for everything from wedding receptions to shaking and baling Christmas trees.

Approaching the roll-up door, Tori heard, "There you are."

She looked up at Gloriana's voice to find her standing just outside the wide opening.

Smiling, she hurried to hug her friend. "Look at you." Tori set a hand on Gloriana's baby bump. "I can't wait to find out what you're having."

"Me either." Gloriana hooked her arm through Tori's as they continued into the barn where lights twinkled amid the rafters and country music filled the air, along with the aroma of smoked meat and the conversations of both longtime and new friends.

"I see Justin's parents made it in from north Texas." Tori eyed her friend.

"Yes, and I'm pretty sure both his mama and mine are plotting to go shopping just as soon as they find out whether we're having a boy or a girl."

"Tori?"

Gloriana released her and Tori turned at Micah's voice. When she did, the warmth in his dark gaze had her heart skipping a beat.

"Would you like a bottle of water or some hot cider?" He pointed to the drink table adorned with pumpkins and faux fall leaves across the way.

"Hot cider sounds delicious. Thank you." Returning her attention to her friend, she discovered Gloriana staring at her with a knowing expression. "What?"

"Care to tell me what's going on with you and Micah?" Could Gloriana's eyebrows arch any higher?

"What do you mean? We're friends. Just like always." Except for her growing attraction to him. And thoughts that went way beyond friendship.

"Tori, honey, are you forgetting who you're talking to? Something has changed between you two. The way you looked at each other just now. I mean, if I didn't know better, I'd think you were a couple."

"Stop overreacting. He's just being nice." Tori lowered her voice. "Are you forgetting he's my late husband's brother?"

"So what? That can't be any weirder than my daughter's adopted father marrying her biological mother."

"But neither of you knew that when you were falling in love. Besides, even if I *might* feel a twinge of something more than friendship for Micah—which I'm not saying I do—that doesn't mean he feels the same way about me."

Her friend's eyes darted across the room to the man in question. "The guy just asked you what you wanted to drink."

"He was being polite." Tori couldn't help rolling her eyes. "Now, can we please change the subject before he comes back here?"

"In that case, I saw you in church last week." Gloriana's brown eyes bore into her. "Does that mean you've come to your senses and changed your tune about God?"

"Not really." She recalled the comment Micah had made the day of Aiden's birthday party. That she could lead by example or expect Aiden to do something she wasn't willing to do herself. So, while her heart wasn't necessarily in it, she didn't want to deter Aiden. "But I also don't want to discourage my son from growing in his relationship with the Lord."

Her friend heaved a sigh. "It's a starting point, I suppose."

"Excuse me." Justin, Gloriana's husband, took hold of his wife's elbow. "Can I borrow you for a minute?"

"Of course." Smiling like a lovesick teenager, Gloriana cast her a glance. "We'll talk later."

Tori was sure they would. Yet, while she loved her friend dearly, she was happy to see her leave.

"Here you go." Micah handed her a steaming cup. "Be careful, it's extremely hot."

She reached for it, welcoming the warmth on her chilled fingers. "Thank you." Inhaling the delightfully spicy aroma, she watched as he took a sip of his. "How is it?"

"Really good. Once it cools down, anyway."

"Hey, Micah!"

They turned to find Gabriel flanked by Brady and Jake, waving Micah over.

"No telling what that's about." Micah looked her way. "You okay?"

"Of course." It wasn't like he had to babysit her.

If I didn't know better, I'd think you were a couple.

Gloriana was wrong. Micah always put others first. That's just who he was.

"I'll grab us a couple of seats," he said as he walked away.

"Okay." She watched him go, until she saw a grinning Jillian coming her way.

"Have you ever noticed that whenever those guys are together, they turn into teenagers again?"

"They sure do." Tori took a sip of her drink, savoring the flavors of apple and cinnamon as she looked around the barn. "Have you ever been back here before?"

"Yes. I was actually at Hawkins and Annalise's wedding."

"That's right. You were Gabriel's date."

Jillian nodded. "Back before my world was upended."

"And now the two of you are married." Tori couldn't help smiling.

"I had a lot to overcome. Just like you. But with God, nothing is impossible." Eyeing the men, Jillian said, "I haven't seen you in a while." She turned her attention to Tori. "How are you doing?"

"Better. Still struggling, but my head is in a slightly better place." Thanks to Micah. Sometimes she felt as though he knew her better than she knew herself.

"I'm glad to hear that." Jillian tucked a lock of her auburn hair behind one ear. "I've been praying for you. Sometimes we just need a change in perspective. You know, to stop dwelling on what we've lost and focus on what we have."

Tori stared at her friend. That was exactly what she had been doing. She'd been so focused on what had been taken from her that she'd forgotten what she'd had. Aiden. Good friends. A family with Peggy and Micah.

Micah… It was getting harder and harder to deny that what she felt for him was more than friendship. But that didn't mean he felt the same way. Micah was the kind of guy who always looked after others. Especially his friends. So how could she know if what he felt for her was simply friendship or something more? Did she even dare hope for something more?

"This is gonna be awesome!"

From his perch near the top of a metal extension ladder late the next afternoon, Micah couldn't help smiling at Aiden's enthusiasm. After returning from the party last night—where everyone had learned Justin and Gloriana were having a baby girl—Micah and Tori had headed straight for the metal building that had once housed goats, a donkey and countless other critters he and Joel had raised when they were kids.

Inside the small barn that was now used for storage, they'd located enough lights to illuminate all of Hope Crossing, along with extension cords and his father's designs—drawings, and even notes on how to electrify everything—fueling their excitement. It had made it difficult to sleep with so many ideas tumbling around his head.

Or, perhaps, it was because of the way Tori had looked at him when she'd mentioned recreating one of his father's displays. Her eyes had sparkled in the glow of all the lights at the Christmas tree farm, making it impossible for him to say no.

Over breakfast this morning, they'd determined what they were willing to attempt, then, after church—which Tori had once again attended—they'd changed clothes and grabbed a quick lunch before hauling everything from the barn to the front yard.

Now, as the sun began to set, they'd wrapped the trunks and limbs of the three crepe myrtles in front of the garage with multicolored lights, lined the drive and walkway with white C9 bulbs, and he was currently working on outlining the eaves along front of the house with white icicle lights.

"Micah, if you fall, I'm going to hurt you."

He glanced down from the two-story peak to glimpse Tori holding fast to the ladder. "If I fall, I'm sure I'll do a pretty good job of that all by myself." He couldn't help chuckling. The banter reminded him of similar conversations his folks used to have when he was a kid and he, Joel, Mom and Dad had made a family affair of hanging Christmas lights. Executing whatever design his father had come up with had been a high point for the man each and every year. Until a heart attack had claimed his life eight years ago, days after his sixtieth birthday.

Yet another reason why Micah had ultimately decided to separate from the marines. Though Joel was the one who'd promised he'd come back to look after their mother and Tori, he'd never followed through. Even after Aiden had been born. That had always annoyed Micah. Then, suddenly, Joel was gone, too.

Inserting the wire into the clip, he thought back to the party last night. The way his friends had razzed him for being so attentive to Tori, claiming he was acting like a lovestruck teenager and making them look bad. Annoyed, he'd told them to grow up, reminding them Tori was his sister-in-law.

You share the same last name, not DNA, Gabriel had been quick to point out.

As if that made a difference. Tori only saw Micah as a friend. Always had, always would.

With that section of lights secured, he descended the ladder, moved it over several feet before ascending it once again. He repeated the process a few more times until the front of the house was completed.

The sun had disappeared by the time he descended the ladder for the final time, adding a slight chill to the night air. He stepped back to survey his work. "What do you think, Aiden?"

"It looks *great*!" The kid thrust his arms into the air, which encouraged Lizzie to leap alongside him and bark.

"It really does." Moving beside Micah, her sweatshirt-covered arms crossed, Tori nudged him with her elbow.

"But watching you on that ladder gave me heart palpitations."

He cast her a curious look. "Why? I'm a firefighter. I know my way around a ladder."

"I suppose." She shrugged, still holding herself. "But I'd never forgive myself if something happened to you. This was my idea, after all."

"And a really good one at that." He admired their work thus far. "Things are looking mighty festive. I think Mom's going to be pleased." After church, she'd come home only long enough to change clothes before heading to Hank's where they were repainting the kitchen and living room.

"She sure is spending a lot of time at Hank's." Tori brushed a strand of hair away from her face. "I still think things are getting serious between them."

As much as he hated to admit it… "I do, too. Every time she talks about whatever project they're working on at his place, she sounds like a lovesick schoolgirl."

"Aww, I think it's cute. After all, one is never too old to find their happily-ever-after."

"What about your happily-ever-after?" The words were out of his mouth before he realized what he'd said. What if she thought he meant with him? Or worse, that he was encouraging her to find love with someone else?

But wasn't that what he wanted?

Not in his heart of hearts. Yes, he wanted Tori to be happy. To have someone who cared for her and made her happy. Yet he couldn't seem to let go of the part of him that longed to be that man.

Her pretty blue eyes met his. "I've dreamed of that since I was a little girl watching princess movies. But things didn't play out the way I thought they would. And while I'm not saying never, I'm no longer the teenager who allowed herself to be swept off her feet by the first guy who showed any real interest in her. I want someone I know will always be there for me. Whose love I will never doubt."

Micah gulped, wishing he could be that man. Just the way he had before Joel had stolen Tori's heart. But, just like now, Tori had only thought of him as her friend.

"As it should be." Turning, he cleared his throat. "So, uh, all we have left to do is put the lights on that live oak." He nodded in the direction of the sprawling tree with low-hanging limbs that stretched across the yard. "Would you prefer we do it now or tomorrow?

"Depends."

"On?"

She arched a brow. "You're the one who's been going up and down the ladder while Aiden and I stood around doing nothing. What would you prefer?"

"You weren't doing nothing. You were supervising. Making sure I didn't topple from that ladder. Or ready to catch me if I did."

Puffing out a laugh, she shook her head. "You are such a dork."

"Yeah, well, it takes one to know one." Hands on his hips, he eyed the darkness around the tree he used to climb as a kid. "I prefer doing it when it's dark out. Makes it easier to see if the lights are spaced correctly." His stomach growled and she gave him a curious look.

"Hungry?"

"Kinda." He rubbed his belly.

"In that case, you take care of the extension ladder while I rustle up something for us to eat, and we'll meet back out here."

"You got it." He turned. "Hey, Aiden! Come help me

with this ladder." Not that the kid could do much, but it would allow Micah to keep an eye on him.

By the time Tori rejoined them, Micah had connected the tree lights to an extension cord and started winding them around the oak's massive trunk.

"Come and get it." She was carrying a large serving tray. "There's hot tomato soup in the thermos and I've got some grilled cheese sticks to go with it."

"What are grilled cheese sticks?" Aiden started toward his mother while Micah set the ball of lights on the ground.

"Grilled cheese sandwiches cut into sticks, so it'll be easier to dunk them into your cup of soup."

"That is genius," Micah said as he joined them.

She set the tray atop one of the lidded storage containers. "Necessity is the mother of invention." After removing the lid from the thermos, she poured the steaming red liquid into a cup, filling it halfway. "Here you go, Aiden. Be careful," she added as the boy took hold of it. "That soup is hot."

"Let me grab some chairs." Micah hurried around the side of the house to the garage where he grabbed three camp chairs and rushed back to set them up. Then he motioned for Aiden to sit before eagerly claiming his own supper. "Grilled cheese and tomato soup. It doesn't get much better than that."

"Agreed." Tori filled his cup with soup and handed it to him. "And the fact that we get to enjoy it outside among the Christmas lights, the cool air nipping our noses, makes it feel rather festive."

His fingers brushed against hers as he took hold of the cup, sending a rush of warmth straight to his heart. Meeting her gaze, he felt like that awkward sixteen-year-old boy he'd once been. The one who'd never been brave enough to tell Tori how he really felt about her. "It's the kind of thing memories are made of."

This had certainly been one of the best days he'd had in…well, longer than he could remember. It felt like they were a real family. The two-parents-and-a-kid variety.

Steam wafted from the cup as she released it, her smile on the shy side. "That's exactly why I wanted to do the lights." She lowered her voice. "After losing the house, I want this Christmas to be extra special for Aiden. To create some new memories. Happy ones that will overshadow the bad."

Micah glanced at the boy who was doing his best to keep Lizzie away from his food. "I think you're off to a good start."

"Because of you." Concentrating on pouring soup into her own cup, she continued. "Not only could I never pull off something like this—" setting the thermos on the tray, she gestured toward the lights "—but I'd still be miserable instead of giving my son the kind of holiday season he deserves." She reached for a grilled cheese stick. "Last night, Jillian reminded me how much better life is when we stop dwelling on what we've lost and focus on what we have." Tori's cornflower-blue eyes finally met his. "You helped me do that, Micah. And I can't thank you enough. Aiden and I are beyond blessed to have you in our lives."

The sudden urge to take her into his arms and tell her he wanted to be a part of her life forever nearly overwhelmed Micah. Obviously, some part of his brain had bought into the childish musings of his buddies.

"That's what friends are for." Yet even as the words left his mouth, he couldn't ignore the fact that he'd been happier these past few weeks than he'd been in years. And it was all because of Tori and Aiden. Helping them… Being with them day in and day out… Doing life together had given him a taste of what he'd thought of as forbidden fruit ever since Tori and Joel had started dating.

But looking into her eyes right now, Micah found himself wondering if Gabriel had been right. That, maybe, they could have a future together. And he wanted to kiss her in the worst way.

Suddenly, a beam of headlights cut through his line of vision.

Squinting, he eyed the vehicle pulling into the drive.

It came to an abrupt stop, the driver killing the lights as the door opened and his mother emerged. "Micah Stallings? What have you done?"

Absolutely nothing. At least where Tori was concerned. And, at the moment, he wasn't sure if that was a good thing or not.

Chapter Nine

Despite the lingering darkness outside, Micah was up, dressed, and enjoying his coffee and a microwaved sausage biscuit at the table when his mother came into the kitchen just after six-thirty the next morning.

"You're up early." Wearing her fuzzy blue robe, she retrieved a mug from the cupboard over the coffee maker. "I expected you to take advantage of your school break and sleep in." She reached for the pot and began to pour. "Especially after putting up all those lights yesterday. I remember how much work that was." Returning the carafe to the warmer, she wrapped both hands around her cup and started toward him.

It had been after nine when he and Tori had finished with the live oak. Then they'd had to haul all the bins back to the barn.

Eyeing his mother as she approached, he said, "Since when have you known me to sleep in?" He took another bite of his sandwich.

"Not since you went into the military." She snorted. "Quite a change from your teenage years." She eased into the chair beside him. "There were times your father and I had to threaten you within an inch of your life to get you out of bed."

"What can I say? A growing boy needs his rest."

"I hope Aiden doesn't do that to Tori." Setting the mug to her lips, she took a tentative sip. "I guess the two of them are still asleep. All that fresh air and running around with Lizzie ought to have worn Aiden plum out."

"I thought he'd get bored, but he stayed with us the whole time." Micah shoved the last bite of his sandwich into his mouth. Chased it with what remained of his coffee.

"It sure was nice to drive up and see all those lights again. I hadn't realized how much I'd missed them." Leaning back, her mug in one hand, Mom added, "I'm glad Tori suggested y'all put them up." Watching Micah, she added, "Having her and Aiden here has breathed new life into this big ol' house."

He couldn't argue. Things were much different now than when it had been only him and his mother rambling around the place. If only he could keep his heart out of the equation and restrict his thoughts to the easygoing friendship he and Tori had always shared.

Had she known what he'd been thinking prior to Mom and Hank's arrival? That he'd wanted to kiss her in the worst way. Had even allowed himself to contemplate a future with her.

Talk about reading too much into Tori's comments.

Thankfully, the Lord had prevented him from making a fool of himself.

"Good morning."

Starting at Tori's voice, he turned, along with his mother, as Tori shuffled across the tiled floor in her slippers, baggy pajama bottoms and an oversize sweatshirt, her hair a mess. She was beautiful.

"G'mornin', sweet thing." Mom was on her feet now. "You look like you could use come caffeine."

"That's for sure." Yawning, Tori ran her fingers through

her long locks, urging them away from her face. "I slept like a rock. I can get it myself, though."

Mom waved her off and continued toward the coffeepot. "I need a refill anyway."

Tori looked his way and sent him a sleepy smile that triggered thoughts he'd spent the entire night trying to erase from his brain. "You certainly don't look any worse for the wear. And you're the one who did the bulk of the work."

Grabbing his empty mug, he stood and started for the sink. "Muscles a little sore?"

"Yes. And I only used a stepstool."

He grinned as he set his cup on the counter beside the sink. "I guess somebody's out of shape."

"Showoff." She playfully shoved him before accepting the steaming cup Mom offered her, then ambled past him while his mother poured herself a refill.

Replacing the carafe, she eyed Micah. "What time are you supposed to be at Hank's?"

Last night Hank had asked Micah if he would come over and help him move some furniture and pull up the carpet in his living room in preparation for the new flooring he was planning to install.

"We agreed on seven-thirty." Micah glanced at his watch, wishing he'd said seven. With so many conflicting emotions where Tori was concerned, the last thing he needed was to spend any more time with her than necessary. Maybe he'd leave early and drop by Plowman's for some kolaches.

Returning his attention to his mother, he added, "Honestly, I'm surprised there's anything left to do over there with all the time you've been spending at Hank's."

Pink bloomed on her cheeks. "The man's been a bachelor for more than two decades. And I don't think he's done a thing to that house since his wife passed away." With a jut of her chin, she added, "Besides, he needs your muscles."

Wearing a grin, Micah peered down at her. "Why are you getting so defensive?"

"I'm not. I—" She clutched the lapels of her robe with her free hand, her face growing even more red.

He couldn't stop the chuckle that bubbled out. "At ease, Mom. I'm just messing with you."

She swatted him as he slipped one arm around her shoulders. "I ought to have your hide, Micah Stallings."

"You won't, though." He dropped a kiss atop her head. "I'm your baby and you love me too much."

Setting her cup aside, she wound her arms around his middle and squeezed him tight. "At the moment, that's your only saving grace."

"If you say so." Releasing her, he glanced at the table where Tori now sat. Just the sight of her had his pulse kicking up a notch. "I think I'm gonna go ahead and leave. I need to stop by Plowman's anyway."

"All right, son. Don't let Hank work you too hard."

If it kept him away from Tori, he didn't mind the work.

After retrieving his jacket, he told Tori to let Aiden know he'd play with him later, then continued out the door into the brisk morning air. The sun was barely above the horizon, casting a soft glow in the eastern sky as he made his way to his truck.

Inside the cab, he started the engine and rubbed his hands together. "Come on, heat."

Following a quick stop at Plowman's for the breakfast pastries and a cup of coffee, he continued on to Hank's.

The seventies-era ranch house on the edge of town was well kept, though the tan brick and brown trim did little to dress the home up. Pulling into the drive, he couldn't help noticing that other than a couple of nice trees in the yard, the place was relatively unadorned. No shrubs or flower beds. Not at all like Mama's landscaped yard.

The sun shone brightly by the time he stepped onto the small covered porch. Reaching for the doorbell with the hand holding his lidded cup, he caught a whiff of the sweet aroma emanating from the box in his other hand. And despite finishing breakfast less than an hour ago, his stomach growled.

Moments later, the door opened. "Mornin', Micah." Pushing the storm door wide, Hank glanced at the box. "Whatcha got there?"

He moved past the man to step inside. "Kolaches. Cherry and peach."

"My favorites."

"Mine, too, sir." He eyed the space to his right that was void of furniture, save for an overstuffed sofa and a large china hutch that sat against the wall to Micah's left. Then his gaze fell to the worn textured carpet in varying shades of brown. Oh, yeah. That needed to go.

"Pretty bad, isn't it?"

Heat crept up Micah's neck when he realized Hank had been watching him. "I suppose it might be a little dated."

Hank chuckled. "Don't worry about sparing my feelings. Brady's been on me about replacing this for years. But with just me livin' here, I didn't see the need."

While Micah was pretty sure he already knew the answer to the question he was about to ask… "What changed your mind?"

Hank looked almost shy when he said, "That pretty little lady I've been spending so much time with."

"I expected as much." He knew the feeling of wanting to impress a woman.

Turning, Hank motioned for Micah to follow him. "I'm gonna get me some coffee to go with those kolaches. You need a refill?"

"No, thank you. I'm good." He followed Hank into the small dining area where a wooden table and chairs had been shoved against one wall and were now surrounded by a coffee table, recliner and other pieces Micah guessed had been in the living room. Following as Hank veered right, Micah stopped in his tracks.

While the living room may have been outdated, the kitchen looked brand-new. Cream-colored cabinets, adorned with bronze hardware, boasted what Micah guessed were quartz countertops in a subtle design. Except for the island, which was topped with butcher block in a rich brown.

He let go a low whistle. "What happened here?"

Pausing beside the sink that overlooked the backyard, the older man grinned. "Your mama."

Micah met Hank's gaze. "I knew she'd been spending a lot of time over here—and at the home improvement center—but I had no idea."

"Peggy helped me pick out everything. As well as execute a lot of it."

Setting the box of kolaches on the counter, Micah narrowed his gaze on the man as questions and emotions ricocheted through him. "I know we're from different generations, but it's been my experience that a man typically doesn't let a woman overhaul his domain unless he's entertaining some long-term plans with her."

The older man's cheeks flushed. "I want Peggy to feel at home here. To create a place where she would want to be. Which leads me to the other reason—the main reason—I wanted you to come over here today." Looking suddenly nervous, he cleared his throat. "Micah, I'd like to ask you for your mother's hand in marriage."

Good thing they weren't outside, because the slightest hint of a breeze could've knocked Micah over.

One is never too old to find their happily-ever-after.

Tori's words replayed through his mind. He wanted his mother to be happy. He'd just never imagined someone would be asking *him* for permission to marry her.

"Hank, you're a good man. You've made my mom happier than I've seen her in a very long time."

The man's gaze narrowed slightly. "Why do I sense there's a 'but' coming?"

Micah laughed. "No buts, sir. You have my approval."

He heard the air whoosh out of Hank.

Holding a hand to his chest, he said, "Son, you had me worried for a minute."

"Sorry, that was not my intention. What do you say we celebrate with some coffee and kolaches?"

"Sounds good to me." Hank turned for the coffeepot then paused. "Oh, and if you don't mind, let's keep this conversation just between the two of us. I'd like to surprise her at Thanksgiving."

"Don't worry. Mum's the word."

As they continued to talk, though, Micah suddenly realized that if Mom married Hank and they decided to move in here, it would only be Micah, Tori and Aiden at Mom's place. And that wouldn't be appropriate.

Of course, if Micah got the position in College Station and moved there, the problem would be solved. Except he sure would miss seeing Tori and Aiden every day. Playing with Aiden and Lizzie in the yard. Sharing his day-to-day routine with Tori. He enjoyed that. Far more than he should.

* * *

Thanksgiving had always been a bittersweet holiday for Tori. As a child, the day had usually consisted of only her and her parents, with the occasional grandparent. As an adult, things hadn't been much different. Save for that one year when she and Joel were living on base and he'd invited several of the single guys to join them. That was the first time Tori had cooked a turkey.

After returning to Hope Crossing, she and her mother had shared most holidays with Peggy and her husband, Ralph, along with Joel or Micah if they were home on leave. After her mom and then Ralph passed away, Tori and Peggy had continued the tradition whether Joel and Micah made it home or not. Later, after Aiden had come along, they'd done their best to make the holiday as memorable as possible for him.

Yet each and every year, Tori found herself longing for the big family gatherings she'd seen countless times in movies and on TV. The kind of Thanksgiving everyone else had, except her. Or so it had seemed.

This year, though, her dream had come true. Not only was every seat at Peggy's dining room table taken, they'd had to bring in an extra chair. In addition to the four of them, Hank was there, along with Brady, Kirsten, Jeremy and Trevor.

Since Peggy had been spending so much time at Hank's, Tori had offered to help with as many of the preparations as her mother-in-law would allow. That had ended up being everything but the apple pie and the cornbread dressing. Tori hadn't minded, though. Instead, she'd reveled in the opportunity, feeling as though she finally had a purpose. And having Micah to keep Aiden entertained while she'd worked.in the kitchen had certainly helped. If only her thoughts wouldn't keep straying.

Now as she sat between Micah and Aiden, her dessert plate empty save for a few crumbs of pie crust, while folks chatted back and forth, her mind began to wander once again. Somewhere in the midst of Saturday's party and putting up the lights Sunday, she'd begun to entertain a lot of what-ifs regarding her and Micah. Things that went beyond the realm of friendship. Micah embodied everything she'd ever wanted in a man. His kindness, attentiveness, the way he anticipated her needs. But he'd repeatedly made it clear they were only friends.

"Thank you, Tori, for that mighty fine meal." Sitting at the head of the table at Micah's insistence, Hank patted his stomach.

"Hear, hear," Brady added.

"Believe me, it was my pleasure." She scanned the faces gathered around the table. "I've always dreamed of cooking for a big gathering like this."

Grinning, Kirsten reached for her water glass. "In that case, mind if I put you on speed dial?"

"Kirsten's a great cook." Brady glanced at his wife. "So long as whatever it is can go in a slow cooker."

"You've got that right." Kirsten nodded.

"I wish I could do more with a slow cooker," said Tori. "You'll have to share some of your recipes with me."

"Absolutely."

Peggy scooted her chair back at the opposite end of the table from Hank. "Well, I certainly ate more than my fair share." She was about to stand when Hank hastily shoved out of his own seat.

"Hold up there, Peggy. Don't you go runnin' off just yet." He made his way along the other side of the table.

"I just thought I'd get a head start on cleanup since we promised the boys they could swim in the hot tub."

"That can a wait a bit. This can't." He stopped beside her chair, his smile kind of wobbly.

Staring up at him, Peggy said, "What can't wait?"

"I can't." He reached into his pocket and pulled out a box before dropping to one knee beside the woman. "I love you, Peggy. With all my heart. Will you marry me?"

The room was silent as everyone stared at the couple. Peggy looked as though she was in shock. And Tori felt a slow smile building.

"Hank. I—" Pressing a hand to her chest, Peggy stared into his eyes, her shoulders finally relaxing. "I would be honored to be your wife."

"Sweetheart, you have no idea how happy you've made me." With that, Hank took the ring from the box and placed it on Peggy's finger amid applause from both families. Then he pulled her to her feet and kissed her.

With one arm around her betrothed, Peggy admired her ring. "It's beautiful. Thank you, Hank."

"Can we go swimming now?" Trevor whined.

"Not until we help clear the table," said Kirsten.

"You boys are welcome to go play in Aiden's room," Tori added.

Amid a round of cheers, the boys made a quick escape while the adults gathered their dishes and took them to the kitchen. Once the table was cleared, the men gravitated to the football game in the living room, while Tori, Kirsten and Peggy remained in the kitchen.

"May I see your ring?" Kirsten asked Peggy.

Naturally, Tori looked on as Peggy held out her hand to reveal an elegant three-stone ring with a princess-cut center stone.

"It's beautiful," said Tori.

"Very sparkly," added Kirsten.

Wearing, possibly, the biggest smile Tori had ever seen, Peggy said, "It seems so surreal."

"So…" started Kirsten, "are you thinking long or short engagement?"

"I don't know." Peggy sounded almost breathless. "I guess Hank and I will have to discuss that."

"I vote for short."

They all looked up as the man in question strolled toward them wearing a smile that rivaled Peggy's. Reaching for her hand, he said, "Would you ladies mind if I steal this beautiful woman away for a while?"

"Hank," Peggy began, "I can't make them—"

"Yes, you can," injected Tori. "Now go on while we clean up." She shooed them away.

As the couple disappeared, Tori moved to the sink and turned on the water while Kirsten opened the dishwasher.

"Clean or dirty?"

"Dirty."

Kirsten began loading the glasses while Tori rinsed the plates. "They're such a cute couple."

"They are." Tori stacked the plates on the counter over the dishwasher. "He makes Peggy smile in a way I haven't seen since Ralph passed away."

"I know what you mean. Hank's got a sparkle in his eyes I've never seen before. Kind of like Micah."

Tori turned to find Kirsten watching her with a knowing look. "Oh, no." She shook her head. "Micah and I have been friends since elementary school. He's my brother-in-law." Her go-to response rolled off her tongue so easily.

"But you're widowed." Kirsten bit her lip and wrinkled her nose. "I hope that didn't sound harsh."

Tori waved her off. "No, you're fine." She returned her attention to the sink. "We have a very close relationship. But we really are just friends." Meaning all her little day-dreams of something more with him were foolishness.

Adding another plate to the dishwasher, Kirsten sighed. "If you say so."

"Mama! Mama!"

Tori turned at Aiden's excited voice as three grinning boys rushed into the room. "What is it?"

"Gigi says we can get our swimsuits on and go in the hot tub now."

"Uh-huh," added Trevor while Jeremy nodded.

Looking at the door, Tori saw Peggy standing in the open-ing.

"Hank's going to get a fire going in the pit, so we can watch them until y'all are ready to join us."

"We shouldn't be long." Tori turned her attention back to the boys. "Go ahead and get your swimsuits on."

"Yay!" Their collective cheers echoed down the hallway as they disappeared around the corner.

Once the boys were ready, Micah and Brady followed them outside. And when the dishwasher was loaded and the refrigerator jam-packed with leftovers, Tori and Kirsten did, too.

The late-afternoon air was cool but not cold. Enough to have Tori grabbing a denim jacket, though. And while the boys splashed away in the spa connected to the pool, the adults had settled into camp chairs in a semicircle around the nearby fire pit.

Kirsten made her way to the empty chair beside Brady, which left Tori no other choice but to take the one next to Micah. Once again, she and Micah were together by default while everyone else was a couple. Something that had never bothered her in the past.

Drat these ridiculous notions that kept popping into her head. Micah would never see her as anything more than a friend.

"Any thoughts on when you two lovebirds might get married." Brady smiled as he probed the two.

"The sooner, the better, as far as I'm concerned." Taking hold of Peggy's hand, Hank smiled her way. "I believe we've both learned that life's too short to waste on a lengthy engagement."

"And I don't think either of us are interested in a big wedding." Peggy patted their clasped hands with her free one. "Just a small ceremony is fine by me."

"Might be kinda fun to be married by the new year, though." Hank winked.

"And what about after that?" Kirsten looked from Hank to Peggy and back. "You both have homes. Where will you live?"

"That's gonna be up to Peggy." Hank met her gaze. "As long as I'm with you, we can live in an igloo for all I care."

Everyone laughed.

"I'm putting my foot down on that one," said Peggy.

More chuckles.

"Though I do believe your house, Hank, would be just the right size for the two of us." Motioning to her home, she continued. "This house was great for raising a family, but it's too big for us." Leaning forward, she looked at Micah and Tori. "Though you two are welcome to stay here as long as you need."

"Mom." Micah cleared his throat. "I don't think it would be appropriate for Tori and me to live in the same home without a third party."

"But—"

"One who's an adult," he added.

While Tori knew he was right, his comment had her feeling a little disheartened. The only thing worse than living in the same house with Micah would be living in it without him.

Chapter Ten

~❧~

While Tori and Micah had planned to take Aiden to the Hope Crossing Christmas tree farm the day after Thanksgiving, plans for Peggy and Hank's late-December wedding took precedence, eating up the bulk of everyone's weekend. And with the school's Holiday Movie Night slated for Friday, Aiden's rehearsal for the church Christmas program on Saturday and the performance on Sunday, it didn't look like they were going to make it to the tree farm this weekend either.

While Tori was tempted to park on that and pout about it, there was no time. The Holiday Movie Night was tonight. And now that the school day was over, there was a laundry list of things to do before the doors opened at 6:00 p.m. The cafeteria had to be decorated, concessions and craft areas set up, not to mention the highly anticipated Secret Santa Shop in one of the rooms adjacent to the cafeteria. The event was her baby—having suggested the idea of an opportunity for families to take a break from the hectic holidays and spend a fun evening together some three years ago—so her reputation was at stake. And time was running out.

She was rushing from the supply closet backstage into the cafeteria with a bag of snowy fluff when her phone buzzed. Retrieving it from her back pocket with her free hand, she saw a text from Micah.

Where are you?

Her thumb danced over the screen.

In the cafeteria.

Can you let me in?

What?

Glancing toward the doors at the opposite end of the space, she saw him waving through the security glass. And the warm fuzzies his presence ignited had her feeling all kinds of giddy.

Focus, Tori!

She crossed the space to push open the metal door. "What are you doing here?"

"I thought I'd stop by and see if you needed any help."

How was it this man never failed to anticipate her needs? "Always. Thank you."

"Uncle Micah!" Aiden raced toward them then launched himself into Micah's waiting arms.

"How's it going, champ?"

"Good. Are you here to pick me up?"

Returning the boy to the floor, Micah said, "No, I'm here to help your mama." He looked at her now. "I'm at your disposal. Whatever you need me to do."

"I don't suppose I could talk you into setting up chairs, could I? They took the lunch tables out, but never came back to set up the chairs."

Removing his jacket, he said, "Just show me where they are."

"I can show you," said Aiden.

Micah ruffled the boy's hair. "You can even help me set them up."

"Cool! Come on!" He motioned for his uncle to follow him.

"Thank you, Micah." Shaking the bag in her hand, she added, "I have to add some more snow to our photo backdrop over here." She gestured behind her.

"Oh!" He stopped. "How do you want the rows set up?"

"Movie-theater style."

With a wave, he continued to follow Aiden.

Moving toward the red cardboard train engine with its black chimney, spoked paper wheels and window cutouts for photo ops, Tori grabbed a wad of fluff from the bag. While the train appeared to be traveling through snow, the prelit Christmas trees that flanked each end looked as though they were from Texas not the North Pole. Those boughs needed some snow.

She placed tufts among the branches, grateful for Micah's help. Since returning to Hope Crossing almost four years ago, he'd always seemed to be there whenever she'd needed help. Making her wonder what she'd do if he moved to College Station.

TEEX had contacted him earlier in the week, asking him to come in for a second interview next week. The look on his face when he'd told her and Peggy the news had left no doubt as to how pleased he was. Firefighting, whether doing it himself or teaching others, was his calling. And while a move would take care of any dilemma with their living situation...boy, would she miss him. Micah was her rock. Without him, she wasn't sure she would've made it through these last couple of months.

For I the Lord thy God will hold thy right hand, saying unto thee, Fear not; I will help thee.

The verse from Isaiah had her straightening.

Where had that come from? Because, despite being back in the church pew, she had not changed her mind about God.

Returning her attention to the tree, she wondered how Peggy had managed to cling to her faith. After all, she'd lost her husband and a son within years of each other. Yet not once had her faith faltered.

Now she was about to begin a new chapter in her life with Hank. Peggy was a blessed woman, indeed.

"Tori!"

Her body went rigid at the panic in Rita Davenport's voice. Turning, she saw the PTA president scurrying toward her. And the distressed look on her face didn't bode well.

"What is it, Rita?"

"The bags for the Secret Santa Shop. We can't find them. We've looked through all of the boxes, but they aren't there. How are the kids supposed to hide their purchases?"

Tori placed a hand on the woman's shoulder. "Settle down, Rita. Breathe."

The other woman sucked in a breath.

"They're in my classroom."

"Oh, good." The words rushed out as Rita's body sagged.

Setting the fluff aside, Tori said, "I'll go get them right now."

Thankfully, the next hour and a half went smoothly, and by the time the doors opened, every task had been completed and the cafeteria was filled with the aromas of hot dogs and popcorn.

The movie wasn't going to start until seven, allowing time for families to have their pictures taken at the Polar Express train, grab a bite to eat while the kids decorated their photo frames or were purchasing gifts in the Secret Santa Shop.

Now as she settled her laptop beside the projector that would show the movie on the screen, she saw Micah walking toward her, hands in the pockets of his dark-wash jeans, his red pullover seemingly highlighting the sly smile he wore.

"You'll be happy to know that Aiden is taking full advantage of the Secret Santa Shop." He stopped beside her. "He even kicked me out. Said he didn't need any help."

"Well, I guess he's a decisive man like his uncle." Her gaze never leaving his, she pulled a cable from her computer bag.

"Yeah, well, just so you know, he's shopping for you and me."

"Of course, he his." She unwound the cable and connected it to her computer as people lined up at the concession stand for their movie snacks. "I gave him my wish list."

"Man, I should've thought to do that." He watched as she struggled to connect the other end of the cable to the projector. "Problem."

Stooping for a better look, she said, "It won't plug in."

"Let me see." He took the cable from her and made his own attempt. When it still didn't work, he eyed the connector at the end of the cord. "The plug is damaged."

"What?"

He turned it so she could have a look. "Do you have another cable?"

"No." She glared at him now. "And we can't watch the movie without it." The pitch of her voice rose an octave with each word. "What am I supposed to do?" Folks were already claiming their seats.

"It's the school's projector, right? I'm sure they have another cable."

"Not one that fits my computer. That's why I always carry my own."

He looked at the adapter again. "I've got one at the house. I'll call Mom and have her bring it up here."

"But she's at Hank's. The movie's supposed to start in five minutes. How do we kill time?"

He stared at her for a moment. Then, as if a light bulb had gone off, a slow smile claimed his face. "I have an idea. You stall them. I'll be back as quick as I can."

"What are you—"

He was already gone, though. Disappearing out the door.

Surely, he wasn't driving to the house.

"Oh, boy." She watched as people continued to file into the room, heightening her anxiety.

Then saw Micah enter once again and it dropped a notch.

Clutching the rubber boots he carried in his truck and something else, he said, "Mom's going to get the cord. I need ten minutes."

"For what?" she asked as he walked away.

She watched him continue onto the stage and disappear behind the curtain. What was he up to?

As the room filled, Tori retrieved the microphone from the stage, her heart pounding. Turning on the device, she said, "Merry Christmas, everyone!"

A chorus echoed a similar response.

Pacing, she continued. "Are you all having a good time so far?"

Heads bobbed amid a resounding, "Yes."

She asked for a show of hands as to how many kids had finished their Christmas shopping and if they'd gotten their snacks.

Suddenly, a collective gasp echoed from the crowd, followed by multiple children saying, "Santa."

"What?" she asked them.

Pointing to the stage, they repeated, "Santa."

She turned as Micah peered from behind the curtain wearing a Santa suit, complete with a white beard and those familiar boots. Making her heart swell with myriad emotions she wouldn't be ready to unpack anytime soon.

Clearing her throat, she said, "Okay, Santa. The jig is up. Come on out."

He strolled from behind the curtain, waving as the children cheered.

Motioning for them to pipe down, she said, "What brings you to our Holiday Movie Night, Santa?"

"Movie night?" Behind the white beard, his brow furrowed. "I thought this was a dance."

"No." She slowly shook her head. "We're going to watch a movie."

"But I brought my own music and everything."

What was this man up to? "You did, huh?"

Nodding, he eyed the crowd. "You kids want to see Santa dance?"

Naturally, their response was overwhelming.

Santa Micah sent her a wink that seemed to say, *Trust me.*

"Okay, Santa. It looks like the stage is yours."

Moments later, Zach Williams was belting out "Run, Run, Rudolph" from a portable speaker while Micah cut a rug, even doing a little breakdancing, much to the delight of students and parents alike. And by the time the song was over, a grinning Peggy was waiting with the cable, an equally amused Hank at her side.

When the song ended, Tori again took to the mic. "Let's give Santa a big round of applause." She clapped right along with everyone else.

Micah bowed and waved amid the standing ovation before he disappeared behind the curtain once again.

Tori offered everyone a final opportunity to grab some

popcorn before the movie started and then hurried to re-trieve the cable from Peggy. "You're a life saver. Thank you so much."

"Oh, honey, it was worth it. I haven't seen Micah cut loose like that in a long time."

"He was certainly a hit. Now, I need to get this movie started."

Minutes later, the lights dimmed and a hush fell over the room as the movie began.

Breathing a sigh of relief, Tori turned to find the Micah she was used to seeing standing alongside his mother and Hank, looking as handsome as ever. The man had been a hero to her more times than she could count. And tonight was no exception. He was everything she'd ever wanted in a man, and so much more. But did she dare tell him how she felt?

Just then the sound of more than one pager went off.

She saw Micah silence his and say a quick goodbye to Peggy and Hank. Then he waved to her before starting for the door, one of the dads—another volunteer firefighter—on his heels. Leaving her with jumbled emotions as well as the certainty that whatever it was she felt for him was more than just friendship.

Micah filed into the wooden pew Sunday evening be-hind Hank, Mom and Tori before easing onto the cushioned seat beside Tori. Lifting his gaze, he took in the festive decorations stretching across the stage. Poinsettias in red and white graced the steps in front of the pulpit, while a silhouetted nativity sat on one side of the platform and a Christmas tree with hundreds of white lights twinkled near the piano opposite. Wreaths trimmed with red ribbon adorned the stained-glass windows along the walls of the sanctuary, carrying the warmth of the season throughout the entire space.

He'd just gotten comfortable when he felt a heavy hand on his shoulder.

"Impressive performance at the school the other night."

He looked up to find Jake Walker grinning down at him. "For an old guy, you've got the moves."

"Who are you calling old?" Standing, Micah glanced around, hoping there were no children nearby. "And you must be mistaken. That wasn't me. It was my, um, alter ego." Nonetheless, Micah cringed at the memory. He'd seen the Santa suit backstage while hunting for something earlier yet hadn't given it a second thought. Until Tori had started fretting about the delay the damaged cable had caused. In that moment, he'd recalled the dances he and Joel had practiced on end when they were teenagers. In trying to outdo each other, they'd both mastered some pretty good moves. Moves Micah hadn't attempted in years. But on Friday night, it had seemed like a good idea. Thankfully, he hadn't embarrassed himself too much. Though he'd paid for it the next day when his muscles launched a protest.

Yet he would do it again in a heartbeat. Whatever it took to ease Tori's distress and take away her worries.

"In that case," his friend began, "your secret's safe with me."

As Jake ambled away, Micah reclaimed his seat as more and more people filed into the sanctuary. While Tori and his mother chatted beside him, he stared at the stage, his thoughts returning to Friday night and the school cafeteria. The way Tori had looked at him when he'd reappeared after his impromptu performance. A look that had held more than just gratitude. Or maybe that was just wishful thinking on his part.

Now as he ran his palms over his denim-covered thighs, he was thankful for the fire call that had given him a reason to escape. And that Hank had asked him to help lay the new flooring at his place on Saturday. Whatever it took to create some distance between him and Tori. Because, even if—by some stretch of his imagination—she had begun to think of him as more than a friend, it would never work. Not as long as she couldn't put her faith and trust in the One who'd sent His own son to die for our sins so that we could have hope. Micah's faith was too important to him. If he ever found a woman he wanted to build a life with, she would need to share that same faith.

Notes of "Oh Come, All Ye Faithful" reverberated from the piano, redirecting his thoughts. And as the children's choir filed into the auditorium, Micah searched for Aiden. His heart swelled when he spotted the boy wearing the red button-down shirt his mother had purchased for the event. Jeremy was in front of Aiden, while Trevor followed him. The three of them had built quite the friendship. A good thing since they would soon be related, albeit by marriage.

The thought of his mother's upcoming wedding on the thirtieth of this month knotted Micah's gut. He needed to find another place to live, but where that would be hinged on his interview this Wednesday. If they offered him the position, it was a given he'd find a place in College Station. If he didn't get the position… Well, that would be a little trickier. Rentals in Hope Crossing were virtually nonexistent. The best he could hope for was something in Brenham or Arborville. Though Brenham would be the logical choice since he worked there. But they didn't have a volunteer fire department, so he'd no longer be able to serve in that capacity. And neither town would afford him the luxury of being readily available to help Tori and Aiden. At least in College Station he'd be doing something he loved.

Tori's hand on his arm had him looking her way. Her smile was wide as her gaze remained on her son. Man, she was beautiful in that red sweater.

"Do you think he's still nervous?" she asked.

Aiden had expressed concern earlier because he'd mixed up the words in one of the songs at rehearsal yesterday.

Leaning closer, Micah inhaled Tori's sweet fragrance. "If he is, he's hiding it well."

Moments later, the pastor greeted everyone and reminded them of the gathering in the youth barn afterward for refreshments. Then, as he left the podium, the lights dimmed in the sanctuary, highlighting the stage.

Over the next twenty minutes, the hope of Christmas played out through song and narration. When it was over, the children were allowed to join their parents as the pastor again took the stage.

With Aiden between them, Micah watched Tori from the corner of his eye as Pastor began to speak. As he talked of Jesus's humble arrival, it was evident that Tori wasn't interested. Her expression was such that it was almost as though she was daring the pastor to tell her something she didn't already know, or something that would change her opinion of God.

And it broke Micah's heart. That she thought she could carry the burdens of this world on her petite shoulders. Or worse, that she could rely on Micah to do it for her.

By being there for her and helping her however he could, was he enabling her?

No. At least, he didn't think so. He hoped he was showing her the love of Christ through his actions.

"You know, we tend to think of Jesus as this baby in a

manger." The pastor motioned to the nativity scene. "Or the Jesus we see with His arms stretched out on the cross when He died for our sins. But we forget about the thirty-three years He walked this earth between here—" he again gestured to the manger scene "—and there." He raised his arm to point to the empty cross over the baptismal.

"Jesus came to earth to live a human life. He experienced the same things we do. Hunger. Physical pain. He knew the joy of celebrating with friends at a wedding and weeping after losing someone He loved. Jesus was even homeless. In both Matthew and Luke, he tells us, 'Foxes have holes, and birds of the air have nests; but the Son of man hath not where to lay his head.'"

The pastor paused. "Folks, we all enjoy this most wonderful time of year. The festivities, food and fun. But let's not get so caught up in those things that we forget Jesus was born in a barn. His family had to flee to another country because Herod wanted to kill Him." Pastor shook his head. "Jesus didn't have an easy life. And He died a horrible death, all because God loves us with an unfathomable love. Won't you pray with me."

As Micah bowed his head, he heard Tori say, "Excuse me," as she whisked past him into the aisle. Was that a sniff he heard?

He opened one eye, thinking she'd been as moved by the message as he had and was going to talk with the pastor. Instead of heading toward the altar, though, she went in the opposite direction. Micah glanced up the aisle as she slipped through the back door of the sanctuary. And the pain her actions brought to his heart was unlike anything he'd ever experienced before.

Chapter Eleven

Tori couldn't escape fast enough. Once outside the sanctuary, she hurried across the foyer to the empty ladies' room, rushed into a stall and locked the door behind her. Tears streamed down her face as she leaned against the partition to stare at the ceiling. She'd been so wrong. So, so wrong, painting God as this wretched character who delighted in inflicting pain on her. And yet, His only son had known pain far beyond anything she'd endured.

Shame washed over her in droves. The way she'd railed at God now tormented her. She was surprised He hadn't struck her down.

"Tori?"

She froze at Jillian's voice.

"I know you're in here. I just wanted to make sure you're all right. Or if you needed someone to talk to."

Though Tori tried to be as quiet as possible, a sob escaped.

"Perhaps we could slip into one of the empty classrooms and talk," she heard Jillian say.

Pressing a hand to her mouth, Tori blinked countless times. The service would be letting out any moment and the bathroom would be inundated.

She straightened and unlocked the door. Crossing to the sinks, she grabbed a handful of tissues. "Okay."

After making sure the coast was clear, they exited the restroom and continued silently down the hallway that led to the classrooms, slipping into the first one they came to.

Jillian held the door open and allowed Tori inside first.

While Jillian closed the door, Tori moved to the opposite end of the room filled with rows of chairs, arms wrapped around her torso as more tears fell. "I'm a terrible person, Jillian. I've been blaming God for every bad thing that's happened in my life."

"I know. And I understand."

Of course, she did. The woman had been assaulted while jogging in Dallas almost two years ago and had conceived a child as a result of the attack.

"I thought He'd turned His back on me," Tori went on, "but it was me who turned my back on Him. I was so angry over everything I've lost. *My* husband. *My* home. I made it all about me. Not once during these last couple of months did I stop to consider what Jesus willingly gave up for me." She blew her nose. "What the pastor said just now. It hit me like a ton of bricks." She sniffed. "I've been so selfish. How could God possibly love me after what I've done?"

"Because of grace." The other woman moved closer. "Let me ask you this. What if, someday, when Aiden is older, he comes to you and says he hates you. That you're a horrible mother and he doesn't want anything to do with you anymore."

More tears fell at the mental image Jillian painted.

"If that happened," Jillian continued, "would you wash your hands of Aiden and stop loving him?"

Tori glared at her friend. "Of course not. I'd pray that he'd have a change of heart. That he'd ask me to forgive him and we'd be reconciled."

The corners of Jillian's mouth tilted ever so slightly. "That's exactly what God has been doing with you, Tori."

She blinked at a feverish pace. Jillian was right. God's love was never-ending. Meaning He still loved her.

Moving closer, Jillian slipped an arm around Tori's shoulders. "We're not called to understand everything that happens in our lives. We're called to trust Him with our lives, come what may."

Tori shook her head. "I haven't done that in a very long time. But I think I'm ready to try again."

"Then tell him," her friend encouraged.

So, she did. And when they emerged from the classroom some time later, Tori didn't care that her makeup had probably washed away with her tears. How could she when that hefty load of anger and frustration she'd been carrying around since the fire, if not before, was finally gone. God could shoulder her burdens far better than she could. Something she'd known all along yet pride had kept her from acknowledging it.

After Jillian texted her husband, Gabriel, and learned that he and Micah had collected their things from the sanctuary and were now at the youth barn with Aiden, the two women walked across the church parking lot to join them.

The evening air had grown cold, something Tori found invigorating.

"It's starting to feel like Christmas." Jillian practically hugged herself.

"Yes, it is." And though Jillian had been referring to the weather, Tori was thinking of the sacrificial love of Christmas settling into her heart. And that made her think of Micah. He was a perfect example of a sacrificial life. Always putting others before himself, never complaining. She'd come to rely on it. Perhaps had even taken advantage of it. But when was the last time she'd sacrificed any-thing for him?

One of the double doors pushed open as they approached and Micah stepped outside, his brow furrowed in concern. Had he been watching for her?

"Everything okay?" His dark gaze moved from Jillian to Tori.

"It is now," said Tori. "We were just coming to join you."

"Sorry. My pager went off. I need to go. Mom's keeping an eye on Aiden." He turned for the parking lot with a wave. "You can catch me up later."

While she was disappointed, Tori determined not to let it get to her. The man was doing what he did best—serving others. So the two women walked inside the fes-tively decorated space, where Tori located Peggy, who pointed out Aiden and the twins at the expansive dessert table.

After assuring her mother-in-law she was all right, she said, "I think I'll join them and get a treat for myself."

Holiday music could barely be heard over the din of myr-iad conversations as she approached her son. She paused, watching as his hand hovered back and forth between a peanut blossom and a frosted sugar cookie.

Leaning closer, she said, "Tough choice, huh?"

"Mama!" He grinned up at her. "Where'd you go?"

"Let's just say I had some business I had to take care of." And now that she had, she was feeling lighter than she had in a long time. If only she could tell Micah.

So, after they returned to Peggy's around eight-thirty, she helped Aiden get ready for bed then read him a story.

Still perched on the edge of his bed, Lizzie between them, she said, "You haven't told me. Is there anything in particular you'd like for Christmas?"

"Yes." He sounded rather somber. He didn't look at her either.

"Are you going to tell me what that is?"

Rubbing the pup's head with one hand, his dark eyes met Tori's. "I want Micah to be my dad."

Tori froze. How many times had she dreamed of the same thing? Micah would, indeed, make a wonderful father. He was a patient, loving and Godly man. But…

"Aiden, that's easier said than done. For Micah to be your daddy, he and I would have to be married."

"That's what he said."

"Wait, you told Micah you wanted him to be your dad?"

The boy nodded.

"When?"

He shrugged. "That day you took me to see our house after the fire and then he drived me home."

Micah had never mentioned it. He must've been too embarrassed. Or afraid of putting ideas in her head. Like she needed any help. Sharing a home with him had only elevated her awareness of what a kindhearted, loving man he was.

Aiden yawned.

"Looks like somebody's tired." She kissed and hugged him. Told him good night before turning out the light. Then she went to her room and changed into a pair of fleece pajama bottoms and a sweatshirt, along with her fuzzy slippers, before heading back downstairs as Peggy arrived home.

"Wasn't that a wonderful event tonight?" The woman slipped out of her coat. "Those kids were so cute. And that message the pastor gave. Very poignant."

"Yes, it was." Tori nodded. "It made quite an impact on me."

"I can tell." Peggy smiled. "But I'm not going to pry because I have a feeling you're going to want to share whatever it is that has you smiling with Micah first."

Was she that transparent? "If you don't mind?"

The woman waved her off. "Of course not. Now, I'm going to go on to bed. I'm exhausted."

"That's fine. I think I'll wait up for Micah, but don't worry. I'll be quiet."

Peggy waved her off. "Oh, honey, I can sleep through anything."

As the woman turned to leave, Tori said, "Peggy?" She approached her mother-in-law as she turned. "Thank you for everything you've done for me and Aiden. For allowing us to live here. For helping me with Aiden over the years."

"Tori, it's my pleasure. You're the daughter I never had, and I love you and Aiden with all my heart."

"I love you, too." With a step closer, she embraced the woman. When she released her, she said, "Now you get yourself off to bed. I imagine you've got work to do at Hank's tomorrow."

"Don't I know it." With a wave, the woman disappeared into the hallway while Tori curled up on the couch to wait for Micah. She must've nodded off, though, because the next thing she heard was Micah calling her name.

Opening her eyes, she realized she was still in the same spot. And he was smiling at her, despite the weary shadows around his eyes.

"Hey, sleepyhead."

Moving to an upright position, she brushed the hair out of her face. "What time is it?"

"A little after eleven. How come you're not in bed?"

She couldn't help smiling. "I was waiting for you."

"Oh?" He looked concerned.

"I have something I want to tell you."

"What's that?"

She wasn't quite sure how to phrase what she wanted to say. But her foggy brain settled for, "I'm not mad at God anymore."

Staring at her for the longest time, he finally said, "That's good to hear."

Why was he frowning then?

"What Pastor said tonight, about Jesus's life. It made me realize that He really did understand. That He didn't have it out for me. And if He says 'all things work together for good,' I need to trust Him for that."

Micah's dark eyes remained riveted on her. "That's right. We need to take Him at His word." He turned away then. "Hey, why don't we talk about this later? We're both exhausted and we've got school tomorrow. So we need our rest."

Though she knew Micah was right, she'd hoped they could talk more.

Sacrifice.

While she'd been snoozing on the couch, Micah had been off fighting a fire. He was bound to be far more exhausted than she was.

"Okay." She stood. "Tomorrow then."

As he started to turn, she caught him by the arm.

He halted, his gaze moving from her hand to her face and back again. "What is it?"

Releasing him, she said, "Thank you for everything you've done for me and Aiden. You're a good man, Micah Stallings."

His Adam's apple moved up and down. "We're family. That's what families do." Then he offered a wobbly smile before saying, "Good night, Tori."

Watching him head off to his downstairs bedroom, she struggled to ignore the pang in her heart. Micah's reaction wasn't at all what she'd thought it would be. But then, he'd been off fighting a fire all night. He was probably wrung out.

I want Micah to be my dad.

Her eyes closed as she recalled her little boy's request. While she'd do anything for her son, that wasn't even in the realm of possibility. Even if a part of her would like it to be.

After his interview in College Station on Wednesday, Micah was feeling pretty good. He'd presented himself well. He also had a lot of experience he'd hoped would play in his favor. But he wouldn't know anything until they made their decision next week.

So he'd headed on back to Hope Crossing and his mother's house, walking in the back door just as Tori was putting supper on the table. Chicken enchiladas. One of his favorites.

"That smells amazing." He set his backpack on the floor and removed his jacket. Save for suppertime, he'd done his best not to spend too much time with Tori since Sunday. Because the only thing that could make Tori more appealing to him was Tori with a renewed faith in God. Now that she'd found that, she was downright irresistible. And that had Micah praying even harder for the position with TEEX.

"Uncle Micah!" Aiden rushed into the kitchen, making a beeline for Micah, Lizzie scrambling behind him as she struggled to get her footing on the tiled floor.

As usual, Micah picked the kid up and tossed him in the air. The way Aiden would giggle always made Micah smile. Something he was going to miss when he moved out. Because whether he got the position in College Station or not, he would no longer be living here once Mom and Hank married.

"Well—" his mother approached, looking hopeful "— do you have good news? Did you get the job?"

Setting Aiden to the floor, Micah said, "They won't be making their decision until next week. But I feel like the interview went well."

She hugged him then. "With all of your experience, they'd be foolish not to snatch you up." Spoken like the proud mother that she was.

When she stepped away, Aiden said, "Mama made our favorite."

Micah glanced down to see Aiden smiling up at him. "I see that. And I'm glad it's ready because I'm starving." He rubbed his belly.

"Me, too." Sticking out his own belly—what little there was, anyway—Aiden mimicked the move.

Man, he was going to miss this kid. They'd always been close, but living with him had deepened their relationship. Yet, if Micah moved to College Station, they'd see each other even less than they had before Aiden and his mother had moved in.

"Let's go ahead and eat," Mom said. "Hank's and my new living room furniture was delivered today, and I can't wait to see it."

Micah stabbed a piece of chicken. "I'm surprised you're not there now."

"Today was the day I'd scheduled to meet with the gal at the bridal shop to try on dresses."

"Wait 'til you see it, Micah." Tori eyed him from the other side of Aiden. "It's beautiful."

Swallowing, he glanced at his mother. "White dress. Long train."

She playfully swatted him. "Hardly. Just a simple yet elegant tea-length dress." Cutting another piece of tortilla with her fork, she went on. "The gal at the store was so helpful.

I'm glad I decided to go that route instead of looking for one on my own. She asked me what I was looking for and then brought me several options to try on. The only downside was that I was gone all day. Which is why I'm going to Hank's after supper."

"Sounds more exciting than grading papers, which is what I'll be doing." The same thing he'd done the last two nights. It was either that or hangout with Tori the way he had been doing prior to Sunday night.

"Aren't you going to play with me?" Beside him, Aiden looked forlorn.

He ruffled the kid's hair. "Of course, I am."

When the meal was over, Micah helped clear the table while his mother left for Hank's. Until Aiden tugged his hand.

"I wanchu play superheroes with me."

"Just a minute, Aiden. Let me finish helping your mama."

Tori looked up from loading the casserole pan in the dishwasher. "That's all right. There's not much left."

"Are you sure?"

"Mmm-hmm."

"Okay, buddy. Let's go up to your room. Give your mother a little time to herself." Not to mention create a little distance for Micah. Did the woman have to smell so good?

For the next hour or so, he got to be a kid again, playing the villain to Aiden's Spider-Man who scaled Lego skyscrapers and rode his trusty dinosaur, all while icicle lights glowed outside the bedroom window.

Micah cherished this time with his nephew. Though he missed spending time with Tori. But what choice did he have if he wanted to protect his heart?

Naturally, Aiden whined when his mother informed him

it was bath time. Not that Micah was all that stoked about grading papers.

He went to his room downstairs and set to work at the same desk where he used to do his homework. A short time later, Aiden rushed in to tell him goodnight. After hugs and kisses, Aiden retreated and Micah returned to his work. Until a knock interrupted him.

Glancing at the clock on his laptop, he realized almost an hour had passed. "Come in."

Tori pushed the door open, looking none too happy.

He swiveled and leaned back in the office chair. "What's up?"

"Why don't you tell me?" Crossing her arms, she leaned against the doorjamb.

"I'm not sure what you mean."

"Why are you avoiding me?"

"I'm not avoiding you." After all, he'd helped her with the dishes. Then escaped at the first opportunity. "I've just been busy."

"With what?"

"Grading papers." He gestured to his computer.

"For two nights?" She sure was feisty.

"I teach high school. They're essay papers."

"Oh." She smiled then.

And something inside him melted.

"I'm glad I don't have to worry about those." She strolled into the room. "Are we still going to take Aiden to the Christmas tree farm on Saturday? He's a little put out that all his friends have their Christmas trees up and he doesn't."

"It's on my calendar."

She nodded. "I hope they still have some nice ones. The last two years they sold out pretty quick."

Clasping his hands behind his head, he said, "Worst case, we pull Mom's prelit one out of the attic and put it up."

Tori looked horrified. "I hope not. Aiden would be heart-broken. He's been looking forward to his first real tree."

"He's obviously never put lights on a tree before." His former fiancée had insisted on a real tree. Then had expected him to do the lights. Talk about an exercise in patience.

Tori shrugged. "I can do it."

Only one more reason Micah needed to watch himself around her. Tori wasn't the kind to ask for help. She was used to doing things on her own.

"No, we'll do it together. Just like we did the lights outside." When he'd almost kissed her. And this time they'd be in closer quarters where he'd be able to smell the sweet fragrance that was uniquely Tori.

Boy, was he in trouble.

After a long pause, Tori said, "So, you're feeling good about your interview?"

"I am. 'Course, I have no idea what the other candidates' résumés look like, but the folks who interviewed me seemed pleased."

She nodded, staring at the carpet. "So, now you wait."

"Yes. I should know something in about a week."

"And if you get it. Then what?"

"I turn in my resignation and start looking for a place to live in College Station."

Did she frown or was that his imagination?

"This house is going to feel so strange without you and your mom here. She was right when she said it needs a family."

"You and Aiden are a family."

"You know what I mean." She palmed the bedpost. "So I started a new devotional on trusting God." Glancing his way, she added, "Since I obviously need some encouragement in that area."

Micah couldn't help smiling. Not only had she had a change of heart, she was serious about learning from her mistakes. That only added to his list of desirable traits in a woman. "And how's it going?"

"I've been spending a lot of time in Job." She shook her head. "If you think your life is tough, just look at that book. It makes me sound like a spoiled brat."

Hating to see her so hard on herself, he pushed to his feet and approached her. "Hardly. You have faced more loss in recent years than many people will know in a lifetime."

"But that's no excuse for my little tantrum."

He touched a finger to her chin and urged her to look at him. And the moment those cornflower orbs met his, he knew he'd made a big mistake. He was close enough to kiss her. And he wanted to. Boy, did he want to. But how would she react?

Lowering his hand, he said, "None of us is perfect, Tori. We all stumble. Sometimes it takes us longer to get back up. But the important thing is that you did get back up."

"Only because of you." Her gaze bore into him. "You never stopped encouraging me. Thank you for being such a good friend."

There was that word again. *Friend.* Whenever she used it, it felt like a bucket of ice water taking him from fantasyland back to reality in a nanosecond. And yet he never seemed to learn. He was like the mole that kept popping back up only to be whacked again.

When would he ever learn? At least once he moved out, he might have a fighting chance.

Chapter Twelve

While Tori had thought Micah would be ecstatic over the news that she had embraced her faith once again, he'd barely spoken to her after she'd told him Sunday night. Until she'd forced his hand. And for a few fleeting moments, things had been back to normal. She'd even thought he might kiss her. The way he'd looked at her had made her feel as though anything was possible.

But just as quickly as the connection between them had flickered to life again, it had faded away. And though he didn't seem to be hiding from her anymore, things still felt strained. Making her wonder what had happened to the easy, carefree friendship they'd once shared.

She'd let her heart get involved, that's what. Allowed herself to dream of something beyond friendship with Micah. Had he picked up on that? Was he aware her feelings had grown beyond friendship?

She could only hope today would prove to be a reset as they frolicked through Christmas trees in search of that perfect one. Then decorated it while holiday music played in the background as they sipped hot apple cider complete with a cinnamon stick.

Okay, so she was getting ahead of herself. And had, obviously, watched one too many of those sappy Christmas movies that had been playing continually since October.

At least they were all up early this sunny Saturday morning so they could be some of the first shoppers at the Hope Crossing Christmas Tree Farm. Yet even as the gate opened, they were third in line with at least a dozen vehicles waiting behind them.

After parking, they emerged from Micah's truck to hear the sound of Christmas music floating on the barely-there breeze, adding to her anticipation.

Tossing the back door closed after Aiden hopped out, she said, "I've been dreaming of coming here for a tree ever since this place opened two years ago."

"So why haven't you?" Tugging the brim of his favorite USMC ball cap a little lower, Micah eyed her curiously.

"The logistics of getting a tree home and inside my house were a little daunting for someone of my stature."

He frowned then. "I would've helped you. All you had to do was ask."

"I didn't want to bother you."

"Bother? We're family." He shook his head. "Sometimes you're too independent for your own good."

"Yeah, well, I was kind of forced to be." *Since Joel was never around.*

She immediately felt bad for thinking that way. Her husband would've gone to any length—and had—for his country. She just wished he'd have done the same for his family. Instead of making her feel as though she and Aiden didn't matter.

"Though that certainly hasn't been the case in recent months." She momentarily got lost in Micah's dark gaze. While it was so similar to Joel's, the two men were nothing alike. If only Micah would realize how much he had to offer. "I don't know what I would've done without you, Micah." A heartbeat later, she added, "And your mother, of course."

Aiden tugged her hand. "C'mon, Mama. I wanna get a tree."

She couldn't help the chuckle that escaped. "O-kay!"

The three of them wandered beneath a large oak tree wrapped with who knew how many miniature white lights on their way to the check-in point as more vehicles continued to pour into the parking lot. Even in the daylight, this place looked festive.

"I don't see Hawkins or Annalise anywhere." Tori glanced in the direction of the beautifully decorated barn porch then scanned the area beyond the Christmas tree truck, before joining the ever-growing check-in line. "I was hoping they might be able to make some suggestions."

"They're probably busy behind the scenes." Hands in the pockets of his worn jeans topped with an olive-green United States Marines hoodie, Micah smiled as he visually scanned the area.

Once they received their measuring stick, tree tag and saw, they joined a few more families already aboard the flatbed trailer.

Minutes later, they were carried into what looked like a maze of Christmas trees in various stages of growth, amid the rumble of the tractor pulling the wagon and the chatter of happy children. The crisp morning air was laced with the aroma of pine. Yet the farther they went, the more disheartened Tori grew.

"It looks like things have really been picked over." Making her wish she'd insisted they'd come out here that first weekend. Not that they'd had time, what with planning

Peggy and Hank's wedding. But they probably could've found some time last weekend.

"Yeah, it does." Micah's smile faltered a notch as he peered out over the tree-dotted landscape. Then, with Aiden between them, he leaned toward her. "The good news is that with a twenty-foot ceiling in the living room, we've got a lot of leeway."

"True, but too small will only look smaller in that big space, while something too tall would be impractical."

His grin wormed its way past her defenses and made her smile. "What do you say we have a little faith and enjoy the experience?"

Sucking in a breath, she knew he was right. Christmas wasn't about perfection, it was about Jesus. Something Micah was good at reminding her of.

Soon, they came to a stop and hopped off the wagon to wander up and down grassy rows dotted with more stumps than actual trees. And the trees that still remained were either too small, too tall or had something else that made them less than perfect.

Across the way, a family of four cheered as their selection was felled, increasing Tori's angst.

"What about this one?"

She turned at Micah's query to find him standing beside a tree that was twice as tall as his own six feet. "And how are we supposed to put the star on top of that?"

"I have a twelve-foot ladder." He grinned.

"Okay—" she perched a hand on her hip "—but what about putting the lights on it?"

He rubbed the stubble on his unshaven chin. "It would be a challenge, that's for sure."

"Tori?"

She turned at the male voice to find Hawkins Prescott striding toward them. "Merry Christmas, Hawkins."

"Same to you." Gloriana's older brother, who shared the same brown hair and eyes, gave Tori a one-armed hug as he nodded in Micah's direction. "Good to see you, Micah."

"Likewise." He nodded.

Releasing her, Hawkins turned his attention to Aiden. "And how are you, young man?"

Aiden peered up at the man, squinting against the sun. "We're trying to find a Christmas tree, but they're all gone."

With a sigh, Tori stood their measuring stick in the dirt then gripped it with both hands. "I guess we waited a little too long to begin our search."

"Yeah, we were inundated Thanksgiving weekend and then again last weekend." Toeing at the dirt, Hawkins shook his head. "Honestly, you all shouldn't even be out here."

Tori and Micah exchanged curious looks.

"Wh-why not?" she asked.

With a tilt of his head and a lopsided smile, Hawkins watched her. "Because we're giving folks who were impacted by the wildfire access to our family tree lot."

"What?" Tori felt her eyes widen. "I wasn't aware of that."

"Then you probably weren't aware your tree will also be free of charge." Hawkins smiled in earnest then. "Follow me."

The hope Tori thought had been dashed sprang to life once again. Sure, in the big scheme of things, her desire to find and cut down a real Christmas tree ranked pretty low. But that hadn't stopped her from letting God know her desire.

"What size are you looking for?" Hawkins asked.

"Eight to nine foot would be good, I think." She glanced

at Micah, who was now carrying Aiden in one arm while holding the saw in the other.

"That sounds reasonable," he said.

Pausing beside a galvanized tube-gate, her friend's brother eyed them once again. "Pine or cypress?"

"Pine would be my first choice," she said, "but, at this point, I'm not picky."

Following Hawkins, Tori felt almost giddy. And when he came to a stop in the far corner of the fenced-off area, her eyes welled with tears as she took in nearly a dozen trees, each precisely what she'd been hoping to find.

"What do you think, Tori?" Micah lowered Aiden to the ground.

"They're all beautiful." Crouching beside her son, she said, "Aiden, since this will be your first real Christmas tree, which one do you like best?"

When the decision was made, Micah stepped in to cut it down. Then, after Hawkins made a notation on the tag indicating it was complimentary, he and Micah carried it to the gate where a tractor and trailer were already waiting.

Unable to contain her excitement, Tori gave Hawkins a big hug. "Thank you." Pulling away, she added, "You just made my Christmas a little brighter."

"Glad to do it." He smiled. "Enjoy!"

"I intend to."

She joined Micah and Aiden on the trailer, her heart full. Strange how something as simple as a Christmas tree could do that. *Thank you, God.*

When they made it back to the entrance, Micah helped Aiden to the ground before helping Tori down. When he didn't let go right away, she lifted her face to look in his eyes.

"My dream came true. Except it was better than my dream."

He smiled then, sparking a glimmer of mischief in his eyes. "And the day's just getting started."

"Can we put the ornaments on the tree now?" Aiden's eyes were wide after supper that night. The kid had been a real trooper, waiting patiently while Micah put the lights on the tree and then again as his mother added some festive ribbon. Aware how bored the kid was, though, Micah had taken him out to swim in the hot tub while Tori did her thing.

"Soon, Aiden. I just want to take it all in for a minute." With Christmas music filling the air courtesy of a smart-speaker, Tori let go a contented sigh. "It's so pretty. And it smells divine." She inhaled deeply. "And the lights." She glanced Micah's way. "They're everywhere. And add a shimmering glow."

Hands shoved in the pockets of his jeans, he moved beside her. "The key to a well-lit real tree is to weave some of the lights all the way to the trunk. That helps create some depth."

She peered up at him. "How do you know so much about real trees?"

"That former fiancée of mine had been adamant about having a real tree." He exhaled a breath. "So I did some research, hoping to impress her." His cheeks heated at the admission. It wasn't until after they'd broken up he was able to recognize how Samantha had routinely taken advantage of him. Asking him to help her with something, then expecting him to do it all by himself instead of working alongside him.

Tori watched him now, a slight pucker to her otherwise smooth brow. "You know you don't have to impress me, right?"

He sure wished he could. But Tori knew him too well. "Yeah, but what about that little guy?" He nodded to Aiden who was giggling as he teased Lizzie with some old tinsel garland. "Like you, I want things to be special for him." And, yes, for her, too.

Her blue eyes sparkling with appreciation, she nodded. "You love well Micah Stallings."

Nodding, he found himself swallowing past the sudden lump in his throat. No words had ever meant more to him. But what would her response be if she knew how he truly felt about her? How deep those feelings went.

"Uh, didn't you say you had some cookies or treats for us to snack on while we put up the ornaments?"

"I do. I'll go get them."

While she disappeared into the kitchen, he told Aiden he'd be right back, then headed for his bedroom to retrieve the gift he had for Tori. Anxiety nipped at his heels as he went, though. What if she didn't like his surprise? What if it dredged up bad memories?

No. He shook his head. If Tori shed any tears, they'd be happy ones. He was sure of it.

"There you are," she said when he returned to the living room. Her gaze fell to the decorative box in his hands. "What's that?"

"It's for you." Moving around the sofa, he said, "Why don't you sit down?"

Though there was an air of caution about her, she eased onto one of the cushions.

Approaching her, he held out the box. "It's an early Christmas present."

She eyed him suspiciously as she took hold of it. "What is it?"

He couldn't help chuckling. "Open it and find out, silly."

"Yeah, Mama. Hurry." When Aiden looked his way, Micah touched a silencing finger to his lips.

"Okay."

Removing the lid, she eyed the abundance of tissue paper. "I can't imagine." She reached inside to take hold of one of the items.

Aiden looked on as she carefully unwrapped the plaster impression of his hand Micah had turned into an ornament, hoping to create at least a close facsimile of some of Aiden's earlier ones.

"Oooh." Pulling it out by the red ribbon Micah had weaved through the hole he'd made sure to add, she smiled at her son. "Did you make this for me?"

The kid nodded. "It was Uncle Micah's idea. He helped me."

"Thank you both."

Easing onto the sofa, Micah pointed to the box. "Keep digging."

She unwrapped the next one, her gaze darting to Micah as she blinked back tears. "This was Aiden's Baby's-First-Christmas ornament. How did you—"

He grinned. "You can find most anything on the internet."

By the time she'd unwrapped the other four ornaments that were identical to the ones Aiden used to show him year after year, tears were spilling down her rosy cheeks. "I thought these were gone forever." Wiping away a tear, she set the box aside and stood. "Thank you, Micah." Before he knew it, she pushed up on her toes, threw her arms around his neck and hugged him tight. "That is the most precious gift I could've received."

With her words warm on his ear, his arms instinctively found their way around her waist. While this wasn't the first time Tori had been in his arms, something about it felt different. Like more than simple appreciation. It felt... Right. As though she belonged there. And he didn't want to let her go.

Sniffing, she released him to look into his eyes. And Micah's heart swelled with an emotion he didn't dare name.

"Do I get a new ornament this year?" Leave it to Aiden to kill the mood.

Tori puffed out a chuckle as she stepped away, though her gaze never left Micah's. "Yes, you do."

Once Aiden had placed his ornament on the tree, Tori added the ones Micah had given her. Then it was on to his mom's ornaments, including a few from when Micah and Joel were little.

Staring at one with a photo of a much younger Joel and Micah together, Tori darted a look at Aiden. "I can't get over how much the three of you resemble each other. It's as if you were cloned."

They continued to work until the large tree was covered with ornaments. Proof that his mother had way too many of them. When Aiden settled in to watch a kid's Christmas show, Micah and Tori tucked empty boxes and tissue paper back into the storage bins.

Tori added a skirt to the bottom of the tree before pulling out the stockings she'd bought the day they'd gone shopping. "Aiden, look at the stocking I got y—" Searching out Micah's gaze, she softly said, "He's asleep."

"You go get his bed ready and I'll bring him up in a minute."

"Okay." While she hurried up the steps, Micah stacked the bins and set them aside to store later. Then he lifted the boy he loved as much as he would any child of his own into his arms and took him upstairs.

Tori had his sheets pulled back, so Micah set the boy on the bed, smoothing a hand over his hair as he whispered, "Sleep tight, buddy." He went back downstairs while Tori tucked the boy in, his heart fuller than he could ever recall. As though something broken inside him had suddenly been made right.

While Nat King Cole crooned "The Christmas Song," Micah eased onto the sofa to stare at the tree glimmering amid the room's dim lighting. Until he heard movement behind him. He glanced over his shoulder to see Tori coming toward him.

"This has been such a good day," she said with a smile as she dropped beside him.

"Yes, it has." Being able to do something special for Tori had Micah smiling.

"For all my drama," she continued, "I've had quite a few good days lately. And it's because of you." She nudged him with her elbow.

He shifted, praying she wouldn't notice how her words affected him.

"Starting with your little shopping day." Her smile grew even bigger. "Then putting the lights up outside. The Holiday Movie Night." She chuckled, a sweet sound he'd never tire of.

Dropping her head on his shoulder, she said, "After all these years, you've still got the moves."

"Yeah, but they didn't used to be so painful."

She puffed out a little laugh that did strange things to his heart.

After a brief pause, he added, "And you rediscovered your faith."

"Mmm, yes." There was a humbleness in her tone, followed by a sigh as she snuggled closer. "If I've learned anything, it's that when the Bible tells us to cast all our cares on Him, it's for good reason. Keeping them to myself was very burdensome. I don't know what I would have done without you."

He twisted to look at her. "Tori, I can't replace God."

"Of course not. But you routinely pointed me back to Him." She cupped his cheek with her soft hand. "You kept watering that seed, even when I was ready to let it die. You believe in me more than anyone ever has." The longing in her beautiful blue eyes seemed to mirror everything he was feeling.

He tentatively dipped his head, his gaze riveted to hers.

Yet she didn't turn away. And when she leaned closer, he gave in to the longing he could no longer ignore. Her lips were warm, her hair soft as he ran his fingers through her long tresses. How he loved this woman.

I can't get over how much the three of you resemble each other. It's as if you were cloned.

The words tumbled through his mind. He closed his eyes tighter, willing them away. Yet they remained. Taunting him. He may look like Joel, but he wasn't his brother.

He pulled back, only briefly glimpsing a dazed Tori before he bolted to his feet. "That was a mistake. I shouldn't have kissed you." Turning away, he dragged a hand through his hair.

"It wasn't a mistake, Micah." Tori was beside him now. She grabbed hold of his arm. "I wanted you to kiss me."

"I'm not my brother."

She shook her head. "Of course you're not. Why would you even think that? Joel is gone. I'm his widow. And it's time for me to move on."

"I have to get out of here." Jerking free of her touch, he

rushed to his room to gather a few things then headed for the back door.

"Where are you going?" A sobbing Tori started toward him, but he was faster.

Seconds later, he was out the door. The cold evening air hit him in the face, bringing him back to his senses. Kissing Tori had been a huge mistake. One that forever changed the dynamics of their family. And likely ruined their friendship.

Chapter Thirteen

As quickly as Tori's hopes had soared, they now plummeted to the ground. How could Micah even think she believed him to be Joel? Sure, they might look alike, but they were as different as night and day. Yet Micah always seemed to think of himself as a lesser man than his brother, while nothing could be further from the truth.

How could she make him see that? Make him realize that she was in love with him. Yes, Joel would always hold a special place in her heart, but he was gone. Yet that hadn't stopped Micah from living in his shadow.

Back on the sofa where, only moments ago, Micah had kissed her with nothing less than conviction, she hugged her knees to her chest. What could have changed his mind?

Headlights shone in the window and Tori jumped to her feet. Maybe Micah had had a change of heart, realized it was him that she wanted.

She hurried through the kitchen in time to hear the double garage door groaning open on the other side of the wall. Her shoulders dropped. Peggy was back. Not Micah.

By the time her mother-in-law entered the house, Tori was back in the living room, huddled on the sofa, doing her best to fight off another round of tears. But the familiar ache of loss had taken up residence once again, poking and prodding her tender heart.

"What a beautiful tree," she heard Peggy exclaim behind her. "Oh, just look at that."

Micah's mother swept into the room, her hands pressed together. Turning, she spotted Tori on the sofa and her expression fell. "Honey." She moved to join her on the couch. "What's wrong?"

The woman's compassion only made Tori cry harder. "He…he's gone," she managed to hiccup out.

"Who's gone, dear?"

"Mic-ah."

"Wh— I don't understand. Did he get called out on a fire?"

Tori shook her head before tearfully telling her mother-in-law everything that had transpired while she'd been gone.

"Oh, those boys of mine." Peggy shook her head. "So misguided. One thought he had to save the world and ignored his family, while the other can't see what's staring him right in the face." She looked Tori in the eye. "You know, when you were growing up, spending so much time over here, I always had a feeling you would be part of our family. I just never dreamed it would be with Joel."

"I loved Joel." Tori swiped away fresh tears. "What young girl wouldn't? He was the handsome hero who swept me off of my feet."

"But he was never there when you needed him," said Peggy. "As a woman, I felt your pain, Tori. As a mother, I'd convinced myself that was something only the two of you could work out, ignoring the fact that you were young and starry-eyed, while Joel's hero complex only seemed to grow." She heaved a sigh. "Joel was the grand-gesture kind of guy, while Micah loves with his whole heart and only wants the same in return."

"I do love Micah." Tori stared at her hands. "These last few years, I've begun to look at him differently. Entertained thoughts that one doesn't usually have for a friend." She felt her cheeks heat.

"Honey, I may be almost twice your age, but as a woman who's recently become engaged, I know exactly what you mean."

"So what do I do?"

"Be patient." Peggy held up a hand. "I know that's the hardest thing in the world to do, but the Bible says that's the number-one trait of love. And then pray. After all, God changed your heart. He can change Micah's, too. Though a stern talking-to from his mother might also be in order." She winked.

"I hate to put you in an awkward position."

"Wouldn't be the first time. I was so glad when Micah went off to boot camp so I didn't have to keep looking at that pouty face of his. I was never quite sure if it was because he thought he'd lost his best friend when you took up with Joel, or if he was in love with you then, too."

Tori hung her head. "And I was so wrapped up in planning my wedding that I kind of ignored Micah. I mean it wasn't like he wanted to sit around and listen to me gush about his brother." Tori covered her face with her hands. "I hate that I've hurt him."

"I know, dear. We'll just have to wait and see what happens. I'm sure he'll be back."

But he didn't come home that night. And he wasn't in church the next morning, either, much to Aiden's dismay. Finally, Sunday afternoon, Micah's truck pulled into the driveway.

Spotting him, Aiden rushed out to meet him before Tori could stop the boy. He'd been moping around all day, confused as to why Micah had not only left but hadn't said goodbye.

Now, Tori waited inside the kitchen door, wondering what she should say or how to act. Her heart was still tattered from last night. Why couldn't he believe that what she felt for him was real?

When Aiden finally tugged his uncle into the kitchen with Lizzie trailing behind them while her boy chattered a mile a minute, Tori's heart squeezed. If she'd had any inklings of doubt, they were wiped away the moment she laid eyes on Micah. She loved him. And knowing that he thought she couldn't love him for the man he was made her so very sad.

"Aiden," she heard Micah say and then watched as he knelt beside her son.

"I'm just here to get a few things."

"What kind of things?" Aiden looked so confused.

"My clothes and shoes."

"Are you going on a trip?"

"No. I'm going to be living someplace else from now on."

"Why?"

"Because…" Micah's gaze lifted to hers and she saw her own pain echoed in those dark depths. Pain that could be so easily erased if he'd only believe in her. In them.

Returning his attention to Aiden, he cleared his throat. "I just can't be here right now."

"But then who will play with me and help me ride my bike?"

"Your mama does those things."

Aiden's bottom lip pooched out. "It's not the same."

Standing, Micah held out a hand. "Would you like to come and help me pack?"

Aiden shook his head. Looking up, he caught Tori watching him. He turned and flung his arms around her, burying his face in her shirt as his tears began to fall.

Stroking her son's hair, she dared to look at Micah. "You don't have to do this."

He stood then. "Yes, I do." He whisked past her and Aiden on his way to his room.

In that moment, her heart broke for her son every bit as much as it did for herself. But most of all, it broke for Micah because he couldn't see how worthy of love he was. And as long as that was the case, they didn't stand a chance.

Micah headed home from school Wednesday afternoon, uncertain as to what home was anymore. For most of his life, it had been his parents' house. Until he'd allowed his own desires to supersede common sense. He and Tori had been friends since elementary school. He'd crushed on her through most of high school, all the while playing the best friend. Until his brother had swept in and claimed Tori for himself.

Micah always wondered if Joel had done that just to spite him. Perhaps he had. After all, Joel had always been about what he wanted. Even after marrying, he'd never acquiesced to Tori's desires.

What a mess Micah had made of things. All because he'd followed his heart. Convinced himself that he could have a future with Tori. He scoffed now. Hadn't he learned anything from his time with Samantha? Not that he was comparing Tori to his ex-fiancée. The one who'd dumped him for someone with more charisma. No, Samantha wasn't even in the same league as Tori.

Under a gray sky, he maneuvered his truck onto the farm-to-market road that would take him to Hope Crossing and his friend Gabriel's house. Well, technically, it was Gabriel's grandmother's home. But since she now lived in the local assisted living, the house was a home away from home for visiting family, missionaries or other folks in need of short-term housing. Like Micah.

He was eyeing a herd of Black Angus grazing in a pasture when his phone chimed through his truck's Bluetooth. And while the number wasn't in his contacts, he recognized it.

TEEX.

With a mix of emotions knotting his gut, he took the call.

"Micah, Craig Dodson here."

"Yes, sir." Micah held his breath.

"After meeting with the three candidates we felt most qualified for the program instructor position, I'm happy to inform you that we would like to offer you the job."

Relief and excitement zipped through Micah. This was what he'd wanted. To get back to teaching and training firefighters as he had in the marines.

"I'm emailing your offer package right now," Craig continued, "so you can check that over and we'll look forward to hearing from you soon."

"Yes, sir." Ending the call, Micah high-fived his steering wheel. This was what he'd wanted. So why was there a hollow feeling in his chest?

Must just be wishful thinking over what had happened with Tori. He loved her. But she only saw him as a substitute for Joel.

At least now he could move to College Station and start afresh.

But what about Aiden?

Micah's heart was still breaking at how the kid had run away from him Sunday. Somehow, he'd have to find a way to continue building their relationship, even though he'd soon be living an hour away.

He could do it. He *would* do it. Getting this position only confirmed that God was pulling Micah away from Hope Crossing. Away from Tori.

His phone rang again and Tori's name popped up on the screen. His thumb hovered over the button on his steering column. Why would she be calling?

He started to answer, but let it go to voice mail instead. Then mentally began to formulate his resignation letter to his principal. Yet as he pulled into the driveway at his temporary home just before five o'clock, his phone blipped, indicating a message from Tori.

With a deep breath, he tapped the icon and listened.

"Micah, it's Tori. Aiden is missing." Her voice cracked. "We've searched the house, the yard, the barn—but he's nowhere to be found." She let go a sob. "I don't know what to do," she cried. Then, as if struggling for composure, she said, "He might be trying to find you. So if you see him…"

The message ended.

His phone rang again.

He promptly tapped the screen. "Mom, what's going on? Have you found Aiden?"

"So you listened to Tori's voicemail. And no. I just got home."

"What happened?"

"They came home from school the same as every other day. He played with Lizzie in the backyard, then settled in to watch a show while Tori wrapped some gifts upstairs in her room. When she came to check on him, he was nowhere to be found."

"Has she called the sheriff?"

"Brady's on his way."

Micah jammed his fingers through his hair. "What about Lizzie? Is she with him?"

"No, she's still here. Matter of fact, her pawing at the door was what tipped Tori off that he'd gone outside. Until then, she'd been searching the house."

Every muscle in his body tightened. "You don't suppose someone kidnapped him, do you?"

"I've learned not to discount anything. Though, after raising two sons, I have my own suspicions."

"Which are?"

His mother sighed. "Micah, that child has been missing you something fierce. Been moping around the house all week. I think he may have gone off hoping to find you."

"What? No. That's ridiculous. He doesn't even know where I am."

"He knows you're living in town. My guess is he's headed that way."

"There's a lot of turf to cover between your place and town."

"Yes, there is. And it'll be dark soon."

"I'm on my way." He slammed his truck into Reverse and peeled out of the drive.

His heart pounded. He'd always tried to do what was best for his family. For Mom, Tori and Aiden. It was why he'd separated from the military after Joel had been killed. If Aiden had left because of him…

He narrowed his gaze, surveying the landscape best as he could. With the heavy cloud cover, things were growing dimmer by the minute. And they were forecasting freezing temperatures tonight.

"God, please protect Aiden. Lead us to him." He thought

about Tori. She must be beside herself. Was she pleading with God, too? Or would she again blame Him? "Lord, help her trust in You."

Turning onto his mother's road, he eyed the cattle-dotted pastures on either side of him, looking for anything out of the ordinary. Any sign of Aiden. Yet it was to no avail.

By the time he reached Mom's place, Brady was already there.

Micah rushed inside to find his mother and Tori in the kitchen while he could hear Brady's voice coming from the other room. Though Mom looked like she was holding her own, Tori's tear-streaked face and grim expression indicated she wasn't doing as well. Making him long to take her into his arms and assure her Aiden was okay. But he couldn't do either of those things.

"Any news?" he finally asked.

While Tori simply shook her head, Mom said, "They're looking at forming a search party."

Why hadn't he thought of that?

He started for the living room and nearly collided with Brady. "Have you got anything?" he asked the officer.

His friend shook his head. "We've put out an APB and are pulling a search party together."

"That's what Mom said. Let me call the chief. The fire department can help with the search."

"Definitely. We'll need all the help we can get."

While Brady rejoined Mom and Tori, Micah dialed the chief as he started down the hall to his room. When the man answered, Micah cut straight to the chase. "We need a search party. My nephew is missing."

After giving Chief Henesy a few details, the man said, "I'm putting the call out now."

A second later, Micah's pager went off.

"We'll meet at the station, then head your way."

"Thank you." Ending the call, he heaved a sigh before turning to leave. That's when he saw Tori standing in the doorway, looking every bit as distraught as she had the day he'd broken the news that her house was gone. Except there was no disbelief, no anger. Only a deep sorrow that tore at his heart.

Taking a step closer, he said, "Tori, I—"

Suddenly she threw herself against him, burying her face in his chest as she clung to him.

While Micah may not have much to offer Tori, comfort was one thing he could give.

He wrapped his arms around her, resting his cheek atop her head and breathing in her sweet fragrance while she sobbed, willing his own tears to remain at bay.

God, Tori may never be mine, but please, bring Aiden home.

Chapter Fourteen

❧

"Ai-den." Tori stood in the front yard amid the lights that Aiden loved so much, hands cupped around her mouth as she again called out her son's name. She waited, listening for a reply before doing it again. It wasn't much, but it was better than standing around doing nothing at all. The search parties had dispersed almost thirty minutes ago, and yet nothing.

She burrowed her frozen hands in the pockets of her heavy coat, hoping Aiden was wearing his. It wasn't anywhere in the house or her vehicle, so he had to have taken it. Meaning he'd probably gone off on his own. A kidnapper wasn't likely to insist his prey wear a coat. That didn't mean Aiden wasn't in danger, though. Coyotes, bobcats, feral hogs and more all roamed this area.

Again, she beckoned her son. And was, again, met with silence, save for a cow mooing across the road. Tears threatened once more, but she willed them away. She'd shed enough already. Most of them on Micah's shirt. He'd always been the calm in her storm. So, despite her broken heart, she'd instinctively sought him out. He would do everything in his power to find Aiden. He loved that boy as if he were his own son. And the feeling was most definitely mutual. Micah was the only father figure Aiden had ever known, which was why she couldn't dismiss the notion that that was the reason Aiden had left. He'd wanted to find Micah.

"How about some hot herbal tea to help warm you up?"

She turned at Peggy's voice. "Sounds great." Taking hold of the lidded to-go style cup, she savored its warmth.

Hank, a retired sheriff, had joined in the search party, too, so Peggy was also doing whatever she could to keep her mind busy and to feel useful.

Beside her now, Peggy said, "The pastor called. They've activated the prayer chain."

Tori couldn't help noticing the way the woman watched her. As if trying to gauge her reaction. "I know what you're thinking." She faced her mother-in-law now. "Yes, I have questioned God's sovereignty a time or two these past couple of hours. But, each time, my anxiety seems to be overridden by a peace that I know could only come from Him." She rocked back on the heels of her booties. "So I'm going to do my best to trust, no matter what happens."

"Glad to hear it." Peggy's gaze drifted to the road as the sound of tires moving over pavement reached Tori's ears.

A white midsize SUV pulled into the drive. And all four doors opened even before the driver turned off the motor.

Tori watched as, one by one, her friends emerged and started for her. Gloriana, Annalise, Alli and Jillian. "What is going on?"

"We heard about Aiden." Gloriana rested a hand atop her baby bump.

"And the search party," added Annalise.

"So we wanted to come and support you while you waited," said Jillian.

"The only reason Kirsten isn't here, too," Alli began, "is because with Brady and Hank both in the search party, she has no one to watch the twins."

Just then another vehicle rolled slowly down the road and, again, turned into the drive.

"That would be my mama," said Gloriana. "Because, as you know, if there's a need, there must be food."

Tori watched as Francie Krenek emerged from behind the wheel, then opened the backseat. Moments later, she bumped that door closed with her hip and started toward them, carrying a large pot.

"Folks on that search party are going to get hungry," she said, "so I brought some chicken and dumplings and sandwiches."

"Francie, you are too much," said Peggy. "How you manage to be Johnny-on-the-spot any time there's a need is a mystery to me." She waved a hand. "Follow me."

As the two older women departed, Tori's friends encircled her.

"How are you holding up?" Encouragement rested in Jillian's blue eyes.

Hands in the pockets of her coat, Tori shrugged. "Terrified when I think of what could happen to my baby boy. Yet strangely at peace when I choose to trust The One who's ultimately in control."

Gloriana's bottom lip jutted as she moved in for a hug. "You don't know how glad I am to hear you say that."

When she released her, Tori swiped away tears. "But I've gotta tell you—" she sniffed "—the waiting isn't easy."

"Which is why we're here." Jillian reached for her hand and gave it a squeeze.

How blessed she was to have such wonderful friends. Not once did they try to talk her into going inside. Instead, they huddled around her and prayed, chatted and even sang, their collective breaths mingling in the night air.

Yet while they did their best to distract her, an hour and

a half later, Tori's anxiety was about to get the best of her. Aiden must be so cold out there. His little hands were probably like ice. And it would only continue to grow colder as the night went on.

Finally, an SUV with flashing lights came up the road.

"That's Brady." Tori's hopes soared. "They must've found Aiden." Her heart swelled as tears pricked her eyes. *Thank you, Lord.*

Not soon enough, the vehicle came to a stop in the drive and, sure enough, Brady emerged as she hurried toward him. She could hardly wait to see Aiden. To hug him and inhale his sweet scent, assuring her that he was, indeed, okay.

Instead, Brady held up a hand, as if to stop her. "Sorry, Tori. I didn't mean to get your hopes up."

"So you...you haven't found Aiden?" Her throat was so thick with emotion, it was difficult to get the words out.

Her friend frowned. "No. However, we're bringing in a search-and-rescue dog. So I came to see if you have a piece of Aiden's clothing, preferably something he's worn recently."

Tears threatened. She was starting to get emotional whiplash. And she wasn't a fan.

Sucking in a hefty dose of the chilly night air, Tori nodded. "Follow me."

After locating the pajamas he'd worn last night, she gave them to Brady then watched as he departed.

Please, God. I don't know how much more I can take.

Peggy and Francie brought out a thermos of coffee and soon everyone was holding tight to their cups in an effort to warm their hands.

Suddenly, Tori's phone rang. Pulling it from her pocket, she didn't recognize the number. But since it was local, she answered anyway.

"H-hello?"

"Mama!"

Dropping her cup, she clutched both hands around the device. "Aiden, where are you? Are you okay?"

"Uh-huh." His voice wobbled as though he was about to cry. And that had her tearing up. "I'm at a lady's house. Here."

Tori heard shuffling. Then a woman's voice said, "Hello? This is Edna Prang."

She knew that name. Ms. Prang had been one of the teachers at the elementary school when Tori had been a student, though she'd retired before Tori would've had her. "Ms. Prang, yes. This is Tori Stallings."

"When I let my dog outside to do his business, he started barking up a storm. When I went out to see what all the fuss was about, I found your son shiverin' at the end of my porch. Poor kid's about frozen half to death. He told me he'd run off, but he knew your number, so I had him give you a call."

"Oh, yes, ma'am. We have been worried sick. There's actually a search party looking for him now."

"Well, you can go ahead and tell them to stand down. I'll keep him in the house where it's nice and warm until you all can get over here." She gave Tori her address.

"I'm on my way now." Ending the call, she noted the expectant faces around her. "He's been found!"

She quickly explained what had happened. "I need to go get him."

"I'll go with you," said Peggy. "I know where Edna's house is."

Tori started for the house to get her keys, the other women congratulating her on their way to their respective vehicles.

"I'll call Micah," Peggy said.

When Tori returned with her keys, Peggy was waiting next to her car. "I just talked to Micah. He's already in that area, so he's going to meet us there."

"Let's go then."

Micah made it to Ms. Prang's house in record time, thanks to Brady and his sheriff's vehicle. Since they'd been searching on foot, it had been his only option.

Springing from the SUV almost before it came to a stop, he rushed onto the porch of the old farmhouse. A wreath hung on the front door, the lights on a small Christmas tree twinkling through the window to the right of it.

Thanking the Lord for keeping Aiden safe, Micah knocked on the door as myriad emotions ricocheted through him. Immediately, a dog began barking inside. A small one, if he wasn't mistaken.

Seconds later, a petite woman with a hunched back and a white pixie cut opened the door, a miniature fur ball yapping at her feet. "Hush now, Ringo." As the dog tucked its tail between its legs and turned away, Ms. Prang's faded blue eyes darted over him. "Micah Stallings. I remember you."

"Yes, ma'am. I remember you, too." Though he'd never had her for a teacher, she'd sometimes overseen things in the cafeteria or on the playground. She'd been a tough one, all right. Hadn't taken any lip from anyone.

"Uncle Micah!" Aiden appeared beside the woman, his expression a mixture of relief, remorse and fear.

"Aiden." His nephew's name came out on a relieved sigh as Micah knelt to embrace the boy. "Do you have any idea how scared we were for you?"

"Now, y'all don't be letting all that cold air into the

house." Ms. Prang held the door wide and motioned them inside. "Come on in here where it's warm." She eyed Brady as he started up the steps. "You, too, Deputy."

"Thank you, ma'am."

At Brady's presence, the dog barked again, but his owner shut him down with a single, "Shush."

In the succinct but immaculate living room, Micah took Aiden into his arms. "Your mama, Gigi and I have been worried sick about you. Dozens of people have been combing these roads and fields looking for you." He smoothed a hand over the boy's soft hair. "Why did you run away?"

Seemingly afraid to meet Micah's gaze, the boy looked all around, his bottom lip trembling. "Because I missed you and was afraid you didn't want to be my buddy anymore after I was mean to you. I had to find you so I could tell you I'm sorry." Finally, he looked Micah in the eyes. "Cuz I love you."

The last thing Micah wanted to do was to cry in front of his old friend, but some things just couldn't be helped.

"Oh, Aiden, there is nothing you could ever do that would make me stop loving you. No matter if we see each other every day or only once in a while. You are my buddy, and nothing is ever going to change that."

The boy's dark eyes held his. "Promise?"

"I promise."

Aiden held up his little finger. "Pinky promise?"

Micah couldn't help but chuckle as he raised his own finger. "Pinky promise." He entwined his little finger with his nephew's.

"I love you, Uncle Micah." Aiden's arms wrapped around Micah's neck and squeezed him tight, making Micah feel a little bit like the Grinch when his heart grew.

"Looks like Tori is here."

Micah turned to see Brady peering out the window.

"Peggy, too," the deputy added.

Still holding Aiden, Micah said, "Your mama is going to be so happy to see you."

Tori's eyes were wide as she raced into the room, seeking out her son. "Aiden!" Seemingly breathless, she took him from Micah's arms to hold him close. One arm around his torso while she pressed his head against her shoulder as she swayed back and forth, her eyes closed.

"My sweet boy. You had me so scared." Finally looking at Aiden, happy tears spilling onto her cheeks, she said, "Why would you run away?"

Finger hanging from his mouth, he repeated what he'd told Micah a short time ago.

Tori looked as chagrined as she did perplexed. "You could have called him or asked me to take you to see him."

"I forgot."

Everyone chuckled.

While his mother took hold of Aiden, Tori turned her attention to Ms. Prang. "I'm sorry we've intruded on you like this, but I can't thank you enough for helping my son."

"I'm just thankful he found his way up here instead of wandering around those pastures."

"And she gave me cookies," Aiden announced.

Mom looked Aiden in the eyes. "Do you know who else missed you?"

"Who?"

"Lizzie." She touched her nose to his. "And she's going to be so jealous that you got cookies and she didn't."

Outside, Brady was the first to leave. He needed to meet up with the search team members. Though he'd already notified them Aiden had been found, he wanted to make sure everyone was accounted for and close things out with them.

Micah drove Tori's vehicle back to Mom's so Tori could sit in the back seat with Aiden. She'd certainly be keeping him close by for the foreseeable future.

Once they were back at the house, Micah let Lizzie out of her crate to say hello to her boy. The pup practically knocked the kid over, she was so excited. Then she sniffed him up one side and down the other, no doubt wondering where he'd been.

Micah hung around until Aiden was tucked in, though he wasn't himself. For someone who was usually unflappable, tonight had rattled him. In trying to protect the people he loved, he'd caused them pain. And that wrecked him.

He descended the stairs and headed for the kitchen, knowing it was time for him to leave, even though he didn't want to.

"Thank you for being here," Tori said behind him. "For everything you did to help find Aiden."

"You don't need to thank me, Tori. You know that."

She nodded.

Yet, as he watched her, he couldn't help wondering what would happen when he moved to College Station. He didn't want to lose the special bond he had with Aiden. Even if it meant he had to come back to Hope Crossing each and every weekend, he'd find a way to make it work.

But what would that look like now that things had become awkward between him and Tori? Prior to the fire, he would pick Aiden up from her place and bring him here. Now, that would mean either imposing on Mom and Hank or taking Aiden to College Station with him.

And what about him and Tori? Could he be satisfied going back to being just friends after all they'd shared in recent weeks? After getting a brief taste of what a life with her would look like? Worse yet, what if she fell in love with someone else?

What will it matter if you're living in College Station?

"I need to go." He started for the door. Opened it. Then turned to see her still standing where he'd left her. Whatever they'd briefly shared was over. It was time for him to go. "Goodbye, Tori."

Moving into the cold night air once again, he knew it wasn't happenstance that he'd received that job offer today. He'd spent the last few years trying to fill whatever gap Tori or Aiden needed filled. Perhaps it was time for him to take a step back. But after what had just happened, he wasn't sure how he was going to do that.

Chapter Fifteen

Micah had come home Wednesday night and pulled up the offer package from TEEX to look it over. Then he'd signed off on it and set the wheels in motion before working up the resignation letter he'd given to his principal today. It was, essentially, a done deal. Come January first, he would be a firefighting instructor once again.

Just the thought excited him. Until he considered what he'd be leaving behind in Hope Crossing. He loved Tori and Aiden. If he saw a future with them, he'd give up every dream he had to make it happen.

But Tori loved Joel, not him. Micah had spent most of his life living in his brother's shadow. He wasn't about to spend the rest of it doing the same thing. He wanted someone who would love him for who he was.

Now, as he wandered around his temporary home Thursday evening, he tried to focus on this next phase of his life. Yet he couldn't stop thinking about Aiden and what happened last night. Micah had never imagined Aiden would do something like that. It tore a hole in his heart, knowing that Aiden had thought he'd done something wrong. That *he* was the reason Micah had left.

A knock at the door had him traipsing from the stylish living room with its wood floor and modern furniture into the updated kitchen where he spotted his mother waiting outside the door.

Tugging it open, he said, "What brings you by?"

"You." With that lone word, she pushed past him. Tossing her purse on the wooden table, she said, "Micah Stallings, we need to talk."

When he was growing up, if he'd heard those words, he'd known he was in trouble. And, judging by the look on her face, the same might be true now.

"Son, what are you doing?"

He shifted from one bare foot to the other. "Is that a rhetorical question?"

"It most certainly is not. But it's cold out there, so why don't you make us something hot to drink and then join me at the table."

"All I have is coffee. Fully leaded."

"Bring it on." Someone was feeling rather feisty. Maybe she shouldn't have any caffeine.

While she commented on how nice Gabriel's place was, Micah waited for the coffee to brew, realizing he'd not told her about his job offer. The offer he'd already accepted.

After pouring a cup for each of them, he joined her at the table.

"You know the position I told you about in College Station?"

"The instructor one?" She blew on her coffee.

"Yes. Program instructor. They called me yesterday, before you contacted me about Aiden. They offered me the job." While he smiled, he felt a tinge of regret. Sure, it was his dream job, but the thought of what he'd be leaving behind—namely Aiden—tugged at his heart.

She studied him for a long moment. "And? Are you going to take it?"

"I already accepted the offer."

"I see." Elbow perched on the table, his mother rested her chin on her hand. "And are you happy about that?"

"Of course. You know I've been wanting to get back to instructing."

"Yes, but after all that's transpired these last few months, I thought your heart might be headed in another direction."

He stared into his drink. "You're talking about Tori, aren't you?"

"In part. But after what happened last night, how do you think Aiden will react?"

Looking up, he said, "It's not like I'll be moving across the country. I'll only be an hour away. I can come home on weekends."

"You think that'll be enough?" Leaning back in her chair, she continued to watch him. And just as he was starting to feel a little antsy under her scrutiny, she said, "Micah, what is it you want out of life?"

He shrugged. "The usual things, I guess. A wife. A family."

"You do realize you could have both of those things right here, right now, if you'd just let go of your self-imposed dictate."

"Come on, Mom." He stood then. "You can't know what Tori is thinking."

"Oh, can't I?" Her gaze followed him. "We're both women and we've been living in the same house for the past three months. I see the way her face lights up when you're around. How she's always on the lookout for you." Mom shook her head. "I'm tired of watching the two of you tiptoe around your feelings. Nothing would please me more than to see the two people I love most in this world finally admit they love each other."

After a lengthy pause, she pushed to her feet and came up alongside him. Smoothed a hand across his back. "Micah, you're good at addressing everyone else's needs, working to make them happy. But what about your own happiness?"

"All right, I'll admit it." He peered down at her. "I was hurt when she fell for Joel. Tori wasn't just a friend to me, she was my world. When she and Joel got together, things just weren't the same. All she ever talked about was Joel and their plans. I was angry that he'd stolen my best friend. While they had each other, I had no one."

"That's why you avoided her for so long, wasn't it?"

He nodded. He'd never come home for the holidays unless he'd known they wouldn't be there.

"It wasn't until I was visiting one time and talked with Tori's mom that I learned Tori was struggling because of Joel being gone so much."

"Is that why you came home when her mother passed?"

He nodded. "You said Joel wasn't going to be there. I couldn't stand the thought of Tori grieving alone."

"And when Aiden was born?"

"I'd scheduled leave early because I wanted to meet my nephew. I never imagined Joel wouldn't be there."

"Micah, you've always been sensitive to the needs of others. While your brother…" Mom shrugged.

"Only cared about himself?"

"I prefer to think of him as mission-oriented."

Micah couldn't help scowling. "His family should've been his greatest mission."

"Yes, they should have." She lifted her mug. "Though I believe he left them in very capable hands."

"Mom, I never meant to—"

"Make Tori fall in love with you?" She shook her head. "No one can *make* someone love them. It just happens.

Look at me and Hank. We've known each other for decades. Yet it's only been in the last year or so I found myself attracted to him."

Silence stretched between them.

Until Mom said, "You know, you were all about bringing Tori back to her faith. Yet you won't trust God with the desires of your heart." Taking hold of Micah's hand, she watched him intently. "Son, for once in your life, *please*, follow your heart. Tell Tori how you feel about her. I don't think you'll be disappointed."

He wanted to believe her. But he'd been burned too many times.

Could it possibly be true, though? That Tori loved him. *You love well, Micah Stallings.*

Memories of that day they'd gotten the Christmas tree and then decorated it together as though they were a family flooded his mind. The way she'd snuggled against him. He could still feel the warmth of her hand on his cheek. See the sparkle in her eyes. Smell her sweet fragrance that had enveloped him as they'd kissed. It had been a dream come true.

Until he'd ruined it. Accusing her of believing him to be his brother. He could still see the look on her face. As though he'd struck her.

What if he'd been wrong? What if Tori did love him as his mother had suggested?

Then he was the biggest jerk alive.

She had to do this. No matter how things panned out, whether he believed her or not, Tori had to tell Micah she loved him.

With Peggy agreeing to watch Aiden, Tori got into her vehicle and started into town Friday evening. Continuing past darkened pastures, she contemplated how different the two Stallings brothers had been. While Joel had confidently pursued her, Micah had been much more tentative. Almost as though he'd felt unworthy of being loved. Though she couldn't imagine why. He was caring, attentive, always putting others first.

Peggy's comment from the night Micah had left came to mind. *Joel was the grand-gesture kind of guy, while Micah loves with his whole heart and only wants the same in return.*

Tori wanted to believe Micah loved her. But she was tired of speculating. And if he wasn't going to be the first to tell her how he felt, then she'd just have to take the lead. No matter how nervous she might be.

She practiced a few deep-breathing techniques before pulling into the drive next to Jillian and Gabriel's. Then she turned off the vehicle and sucked in a final bolstering breath. "Lord, Your will, not mine." Though she was inclined to throw in a little begging, she'd already done enough of that.

Stepping out of her SUV into the chilly night air, she smoothed a hand over the green sweater dress she'd paired with black dress boots. Tossing the door closed, she started for the wooden porch outside the kitchen door of the single-story Folk Victorian. Then, before she could second-guess herself again, she knocked on the door.

A moment later, Micah jerked the door open, his dark eyes wide. And looking way too attractive in a gray pullover and dark-wash jeans. "Tori? What are you doing here?" Pushing up one sleeve, he said, "I was just about to come and see you and Aiden."

Her and Aiden? Not just Aiden?

Tucking that in her confidence belt, she pulled the screen door open to join him inside. "There's something I have to tell you." Closing the door behind her, she added, "And I just need you to listen, all right?"

"Okay." He crossed his arms over his chest, his brow suddenly pleating.

Hands clasped in front of her, she met his gaze. "I was seventeen when Joel swept me off my feet. I was in love with love. And while I kept my marriage vows, I can't say the same for Joel. He lived for the next deployment. The next mission. The military had become his mistress while I was left to deal with life by myself. The greatest gift he ever gave me was Aiden. Yet he has no memories of his father. Only you, Micah."

The lines on his forehead eased.

"You have shown me and my son the true meaning of love. The way God intended it. You never gave up on me. You helped me find my faith when I'd given up." She drew in a shuddering breath, her eyes still locked with his. "What I'm trying to say is that I love you, Micah. And I want to be with you. Always. And for you to be a father to Aiden."

His eyes widened as a wobbly smile formed on his lips.

"Tori, um, before we go any further, I should tell you I was offered the position in College Station. And I accepted it."

His dream job. She was happy for him. But why was he telling her as though they couldn't be together because of it? "C-can you commute? Or, maybe Aiden and I could go with you."

Eyeing her curiously, he said, "You would do that?

"Micah, if it meant I got to be with you, I'd go anywhere."

His smile grew wide as he stepped closer and threaded his fingers into her hair. Then he kissed her, thoroughly and without hesitation. When he finally pulled away, he rested his forehead against hers. "I have loved you for so long. I want to be with you, too. For us to be a family. You, me and Aiden."

Lifting his head, he cleared his throat. "As I said earlier, I was about to come and see you when you pulled up."

The teasing look in his eyes had her smiling. "Oh, yeah? What for?"

He released her then. Reached for the jacket draped over the back of a chair and took something from its pocket. "So I could give you this." Looking into her eyes, he opened the red-velvet box to reveal a sparkling diamond ring. "Tori—" Grinning, he lowered to one knee. "Even though you, kind of, already asked me, I'd like to make this official. Will you marry me?"

Her cheeks hurt from the ginormous smile on her face. "I thought you'd never ask."

He slid the ring on her finger then promptly stood to kiss her once more.

Finally coming up for air, she said, "And as far as I'm concerned, it can't happen soon enough."

He briefly touched his lips to hers once again. "I'm in agreement. Do you have something in mind?" Brushing her hair away from her face, he added, "That is, unless you want a big wedding. Because all I want is you."

"In that case…" She grinned.

In the church sanctuary still adorned with poinsettias, wreaths and a Christmas tree, Micah stood at the altar, opposite Hank, five days after Christmas. He watched as Aiden—clad in crisp dark jeans, a white button-down shirt topped with a black sports coat that mimicked both Micah's and Hank's attire—walked down the aisle with the pillow that held four wedding bands.

Since Micah and Tori hadn't been interested in a lengthy

engagement, they'd asked Mom and Hank if they'd mind sharing their special day. Not only had they agreed, they'd seemed somewhat relieved.

"Now I don't have to worry about everyone staring at me," Hank had said.

Brady was serving as his best man, while Mom's sister—Aunt Judy—was her matron of honor. Opposite them, Gloriana and Gabriel stood with Micah as they anticipated the brides' arrival.

As Aiden joined them on the platform, notes of "Here Comes the Bride" filled the sanctuary where friends and church family had gathered for what stood to be the best day of Micah's life. After all these years, all the life events they'd shared, the ups and downs of their friendship, Tori Stallings was about to be his wife. And Micah could hardly wait.

His eyes were fixed on the doors at the far end of the aisle as he waited for his bride—make that *the brides*—to appear.

Suddenly the doors opened and the two women he loved most in this world appeared—arm-in-arm since they'd chosen to give each other away—and started down the aisle. Both wore ivory, tea-length dresses—or so he'd been told—Mom's in satin while Tori's in lace. And while they both looked beautiful, Micah couldn't take his eyes off of Tori. How blessed he was to get to spend the rest of his life with her. And, if God saw fit, perhaps they might expand their little family. They'd talked about it as they'd discussed their future together.

Since he would be commuting to his new job, he and Tori were in the process of purchasing his mother's house, though the price she'd insisted on was way below market value, which would allow them to tackle some updates as they made the house their own.

As the two women neared the podium, Micah caught Hank's eye. And when the older man nodded, they each descended the steps to claim their bride.

Looking into Tori's gorgeous cornflower eyes as the pastor pronounced them man and wife a short time later, Micah knew he'd never been happier. And he could hardly wait to see what God had in store for them.

Epilogue

By the time the school year was out, the major updates had been completed at the Stallings' home. New countertops and backsplash in the kitchen, cabinets painted white and adorned with new pulls, fresh paint and new flooring throughout had updated the entire place. So Tori had spent the first few weeks of her summer break decorating and getting things just so. And since she and Micah had decided to host today's Fourth of July cookout with their friends, that had been just the impetus she'd needed to complete the job.

"Can you believe how much our lives have changed since I moved back here a little over three years ago?" Gloriana stood beside Tori as they watched the kids play in the swimming pool, her three-month-old daughter, Sierra, on her shoulder as Gloriana tried to encourage a burp.

Shaking her head, Tori said, "No kidding." She watched as Aiden splashed alongside Jeremy and Trevor. "And just look at how we've grown."

Her friend lifted a brow. "You're referring to our children, not your ever-expanding belly, right?"

"Very funny." With one hand atop her five-month baby bump, Tori swatted her friend before returning her attention to the group gathered in her backyard. "Six families, thirteen kids."

"And counting. Jillian looks like she could pop at any

moment, you're due in November and Alli's due again early next year."

Tori couldn't help but smile. "Who knew we were such a prolific bunch?"

"Hey, just because we got a late start doesn't mean we can't catch up."

Sierra began to fuss then.

"May I hold her?" Tori had been itching to get her hands on the babe all afternoon, but until now she'd been too busy.

"Be my guest."

Taking hold of the tiny bundle with dark hair like her mama's, Tori inhaled that sweet baby scent. "What's the matter, Sierra? That ol' burp just won't come out, huh?" Cradling the child in her arms, she swayed back and forth, all the while patting Sierra's bottom.

A moment later, the baby let out a significant belch.

Tori smiled as the child seemed to do the same. "There, that feels better, doesn't it?"

"You obviously haven't lost your touch with babies." Gloriana watched her.

"Apparently, I'm not that out of practice," she cooed at the adorable child.

Just then, a dripping wet Aiden scurried toward her, Lizzie at his heels. "I'm starving. When are we gonna eat?"

"You're going to have to take that up with your dad. He's the one cooking the burgers and hot dogs."

Everything else was ready to go and waiting inside the house. Since everyone had been asked to bring a side or dessert, she'd been able to concentrate on playing hostess.

"Okay." As fast as he appeared, the kid was gone.

Gloriana watched after him. "He adores Micah, doesn't he?"

"Always has. Micah's the only father figure he's ever

known." So it had been no surprise when he'd asked if he could call Micah "Daddy" even before the wedding reception had ended. The news that she and Micah were getting married had probably been the best gift that kid had received last Christmas.

And come this Christmas, they would be a family of four. She could hardly believe how much her life had changed this past year. From her lowest low to her highest high. God had been so good to her. Even when she hadn't deserved it.

Once everyone had their fill of swimming and food, all of the families packed up and headed over to Prescott Farms, where Hawkins and Justin had the fireworks ready to go. Thanks to drought-busting spring rains, they were actually able to have them this year.

Legs stretched out atop an old quilt, Tori leaned against her husband's chest as they watched Aiden and the other kids chase each other with squirt guns as the sun continued its slow descent toward the horizon.

"Happy?" Micah whispered in her ear.

"Always, when I'm with you."

"Hmm." He smoothed a hand over the baby girl growing inside her. "I feel the same way about you." His lips brushed across her temple.

"That's good. Because you're stuck with me."

As Micah wrapped an arm around her, she whispered a prayer of thanksgiving. This was the life she'd always dreamed of. Though she'd had to travel through plenty of hills and valleys to get there, God had always been with her. Even when she'd turned her back on Him.

Yet despite her rejection, He'd brought her a man who routinely pointed her back to Him. Micah lived out his faith in word and deed.

She looked up at him. "I love you, Micah Stallings."

Despite the heat outside, his smile sent a shiver up her spine. "And I love you, Tori. Always and forever."

* * * * *

Dear Reader,

I must admit, I'm a little sad as I write this. Bidding farewell to my Hope Crossing series means saying goodbye to all the friends we've met along the way. But what a fitting ending. Some of you have been asking me for Tori's story since she appeared in *The Cowgirl's Redemption*, the first book in the series. Tori was the classic girl next door. A true friend who always cheered her friends on to victory despite the curveballs life had thrown at her. Until life had become too much for her. Then she'd needed a superhero.

We all need a Micah in our lives. Someone who's seen us at our worst and loves us anyway. A friend who refuses to give up on us, even if they know they might be wounded in the process.

The wildfire in this story was actually based on personal experience. The image of those firefighters lying in the road the morning after will be forever ingrained in my memory. Thankfully, we didn't lose our home, though we had a friend who did. And we were there as people gathered to help her sift through the ashes. Years later, we can see how, out of that great tragedy, came many good things.

As Christmas approaches, I pray that you will remember the real reason for the season. Jesus. The baby in the manger who laid down His life so that we could live.

Until next time,
Mindy